"Are you saying that my son seduced you?"

Lucas was furious, Keely saw with satisfaction. She lowered her eyes to her plate.

"It...wasn't all Tarrant's fault," she lied. "We...discussed marriage. It was my mistake. I thought—" she hesitated painfully "—he meant to marry me."

The choking cough came from Tarrant. Catherine, Keely's mother, gasped, "Oh, my, no!" But by then Keely was so hating Tarrant Varley and his insults to her and her mother that nothing would make her back down.

"Excuse me," she mumbled, and left the table. But a smile picked at the corners of her mouth. She was only human, wasn't she? And she hoped Lucas made Tarrant's life unbearable. It was no more than he deserved!

D0651085

Books by Jessica Steele

HARLEQUIN PRESENTS

HARLEQUIN ROMANCES

These books may be available at your local bookseller.

For a list of all titles currently available,
send your name and address to:

Harlequin Reader Service
P.O. Box 52040, Phoenix, AZ 85072-2040
Canadian address: P.O. Box 2800, Postal Station A,
5170 Yonge St., Willowdale, Ont. M2N 5T5

JESSICA STEELE

bond of vengeance

Harlequin Books

TORONTO • NEW YORK • LONDON
AMSTERDAM • PARIS • SYDNEY • HAMBURG
STOCKHOLM • ATHENS • TOKYO • MILAN

Harlequin Presents first edition December 1984
ISBN 0-373-10749-8

Original hardcover edition published in 1984
by Mills & Boon Limited

Printed in U.S.A.

CHAPTER ONE

PICKING up the phone when it rang that Friday morning, Keely had a premonition, when she heard her mother's voice, that she had some good news to impart. Seldom was it that Catherine Macfarlane rang her at the office, although Keely's boss would have raised no objection.

'You sound chirpy,' she smiled into the telephone when, after a bright greeting, her mother had straightaway said she was coming up to town and asked could they meet for lunch.

'Wait until you hear what I have to tell you!'

'Mr Varley has bought a dishwasher?'

'Stop fishing—he's got one, and anyway, it's much much better than that.'

With Catherine Macfarlane refusing to be drawn, though some of the excitement in her rubbing off on to her daughter, after they had arranged in which restaurant to meet, Keely left her desk and went through to the next office.

'Any chance of my having an extended lunch hour?' she asked of the mousey-haired man who looked up as she went in.

Gerald Cullen smiled a warm smile when he saw her. 'Providing you're not intending to lunch with anyone who's likely to make you change your mind about our date tomorrow,' he replied.

'What, after all the trouble you had getting those theatre tickets?' she answered, half of her wishing she had never agreed to go with him to the play that had been fully booked since it had opened its run. Gerald imagined himself a little in love with her—she hoped it was his imagination, anyway.

5

As she was about to return to her own office, her green eyes caught the way his smile had started to slip. It niggled her, that way he had of wanting to know more—niggled her that having got his permission to return late from lunch she should feel obliged to add more.

'Actually,' she found herself staying to say, with a sensation of being emotionally blackmailed, for all her liking for him went no further than that, 'I'm lunching with my mother.'

In an instant his smile was there again. 'She's coming up from Surrey?'

Her surprise showed. 'You've remembered!'

'I never forget a thing you tell me, Keely,' he smiled, that suggestion there again of his fondness for her which did not sit too comfortably with her.

Gerald, she was recalling, had asked all about her; about her parents, on that first evening he had taken her out some six weeks ago. Tomorrow was to be their second date—though more on her part because she had run out of excuses.

'You told me how she'd recently changed her job, and was now working as cook-housekeeper to the Varleys,' he trotted out. 'As if I'd forget a thing like that!'

'Because Varleys' sometimes put work our way, you mean?' she asked hopefully, Varley Industries had been doing business with G. Cullen and Associates long before she had come on the scene ten months ago.

Gerald smiled a smile that said her mother working for the Varleys had nothing to do with it. And, at her wits' end to know what to do about him and his unconcealed fondness for her, Keely went back to her desk.

But the rubbed-off excitement from her mother had disappeared by the time she had picked up her work from where she had left off. Her typing then became automatic as she fell into a reverie that began with her knowing quite well that she liked Gerald, but that with him being forty-two and divorced with it, she wished he would act more grown up.

Her thoughts then drifted to her mother, and to how happy Catherine was now that she had found a cook-housekeeping job with an employer who was more her own type of person. According to her, wealthy old Lucas Varley—though at sixty-seven he wasn't really old—was a gentleman. Which was more than could be said for her one and only previous employer.

That first job had only lasted seven months, but in Keely's opinion her mother had been heroic to stick it out that long. Though it had not been until Catherine had settled in happily at Inchbrook, the home of the Varleys, that she had revealed the extent of the carping and fault-finding; not to mention the long hours she had worked, for the grumbling family which had been her first venture into an occupation.

Not that Keely had wanted her mother to work at all. 'We can manage on my salary,' she had told her when, her father being dead a year, the crunch had come. But Catherine had shaken her head and told her what she had already decided—and there had been no moving her from her decision.

How different it had all been, not too many years ago either, Keely thought. Her father, not always the best tempered man, had owned a small toolmaking firm in the Midlands, and after her secretarial training she had gone to work for him. She had seen in the space of that short time how badly things were going, but neither she nor Cedric Macfarlane had been ready for the crash when it had come. Her father had never got over the shock, and with his giant pride in shreds, he had grown ill, eventually succumbing to what had been thought of as no more than a bad bout of 'flu.

But with Catherine upset at the death of her husband, and with Keely upset at the death of her father, neither of them had given thought that their desperate financial situation would not be resolved.

By then Keely was working as secretary to a local solicitor, and had been able to tell her mother that settling the estate of a deceased person took absolutely ages.

So for twelve months more they had lived in the large house Keely had grown up in—the fact that it was heavily mortgaged being no particular problem, since her mother came from moneyed people, the Butterworths, who were eager to help.

But when, a little over a year after Cedric Macfarlane had left them, they were to learn of their true financial position, together they decided that the house would have to go to settle debts still found to be outstanding before his death, and to settle debts accrued afterwards. Not that the Butterworths asked for or wanted the money they had loaned, but both being independent-minded, there was no other way for the two Macfarlanes.

Though in Keely's view, her mother was taking independence to the limit when the very next day she had declared that she was going to get a job.

'But you're not trained for anything!' she had protested, thinking to change her mother's mind. For Catherine had been fifty-eight, and had never had a job outside the home in her life.

'Don't rub it in,' answered Catherine dryly, and handing her a magazine, added, 'Just take a look at that advert.'

'Cook-housekeeper wanted!' Her first reaction had been one of horror. 'You can't do that! I won't let you,' she had said. 'We'll get a small flat somewhere, and I'll . . .'

'*You'll* get a flat—but for one, just you,' said Catherine firmly. And when Keely had stared at the determination in her mother's look, she had smiled as she had gone on just as firmly. 'You're twenty-two now, for goodness' sake. It's about time my apron strings were cut. Why, other girls your age ...'

'Who are you trying to convince—me, or yourself?'

Always close to her mother, Keely knew that she wasn't wanting to give her a none too gentle push from the nest. It was just the way it had to be. Though that did not stop her from arguing the point—but only to find that in the face of her mother's determination she was wasting her breath.

So it was that when Catherine moved to London to her first housekeeping job, Keely moved too. She left her job, and took the flat her mother had said she should—that flat in London.

Her reverie took another turn as she dwelt on that bond. Clearly did she remember girls at school saying they wished they could talk to their mothers about simply everything the way she could talk to hers.

Perhaps, Keely mused, that close bond stemmed from the fact that Catherine had gone through such a terrible time in having her. The facts of life had been freely discussed between them, and she had heard all about the 'Butterworth Factor' that missed very few of the female line when it came to having babies. The few who escaped and waltzed through pregnancy counted themselves lucky. For others it was nine long months of permanent sickness, indigestion, high blood pressure and swollen ankles, if indeed they were lucky enough not to miscarry on the way.

Keely's own mother had suffered four miscarriages and had been advised to abandon the idea of having a child. She had been thirty-five when she had found herself pregnant again. But, when she was sick from almost the beginning and had realised her condition, she had so wanted a child she had been prepared to put up with anything. With her previous experience of how easily she could lose that cherished life growing in her, this perhaps being her last chance, she had obeyed her physician's instructions to the letter, and beyond. The result being Keely.

'If being pregnant is as ghastly as it sounds,' said Keely, sixteen then, though the idea of vomiting through nine months being no more appealing now at the age of twenty-three than it had been then, and the risk of miscarrying an ever-present one, 'I don't think I'll bother.'

'Oh, you'll probably take after your father's side,' Catherine had smiled. 'The Macfarlanes never have any trouble, and sail on to give birth as easily as shelling peas.'

Her mother must then have thought that the time had been right for another little discussion. For Keely remembered it had been then that Catherine, trying to be as modern-thinking as the next, had gone on to tell her that while she was aware that young women these days often no longer waited to hear wedding bells before they went to bed with a man, she would like to think that Keely never committed herself to that extent until she was truly in love with the man concerned.

'You can have my promise on that now, Mother,' Keely had replied, aware of at least one girl in her form at school who was already experimenting, but the scruffy-looking youth she was doing her experimenting with was enough to put her hygienic soul off.

It had been an easy promise to keep, Keely reflected as she inserted fresh paper into her typewriter. Though her mother had forgotten that promise until at nineteen she had reminded her of it when coming home at three o'clock in the morning, after having been to what had turned out to be an enjoyable, if rather wild party, to find Catherine waiting up for her.

She remembered the dressing-down she'd been given for, in the first place, not telling her mother she was going to be in so late. And remembered too, how, hating to be bad friends with her mother, some imp of mischief had seen her trying to tease a smile from her for once stern parent.

'Will you forgive me if I tell you that the promise I made you when I was sixteen has not been broken?'

'What promise?' Catherine had asked, seeing no reason for her creamy-complexioned, raven-haired daughter's cheeky smile.

'I'm still *virgo intacto*, Mother,' she had replied with a grin.

'I never supposed differently for a moment,' Catherine had said stiffly as she had ushered her up the stairs. But Keely was sure, from the relief she saw in the reluctant smile she received as she was told not to make a noise in case she woke her father, that her mother had been worried.

'What are you thinking about that makes you smile?'

Keely abruptly left her thoughts to see that Gerald had come to stand in the doorway, and must have been watching her for some minutes. Wanting to tell him, 'My thoughts are my own,' she smiled instead. It wasn't his fault that his interest in her sometimes made her scratchy.

'The three-course lunch I'm going to have instead of the sandwich that was on the menu prior to my mother phoning,' she said. 'Which reminds me—if I don't go now, I'm going to be late.'

'I'd take you to lunch any day of the week,' he offered as she picked up her bag.

'You'd soon have me the size of a house,' she quipped. Which comment had her bringing on herself his unwanted inspection of her slim shapely figure as she darted for the door.

Keely caught his, 'Never!' as she closed the door after her.

Wondering, not for the first time, what she was going to do about Gerald, she soon forgot about him when she reached the smart restaurant her mother had chosen.

She would pass for forty, she could not but think when they had greeted each other and she stood back to see that her fair-haired, sparkly-eyed mother was looking as trim as any younger woman.

'What gives?' she couldn't refrain from asking the moment their order was taken.

'As impetuous as ever, I see. Ladies wait to be told,' replied Catherine. Though her secret was burning to be told, she paused only to make a qualification, before she revealed to her daughter why it was she was looking so on top of the world.

'I'm not sure that this is the right place to tell you. But I didn't want to tell you over the telephone, and I couldn't wait until tonight to come to your flat.'

'Your news is that good!' Keely exclaimed, no mistaking that what Catherine had to impart was anything but good news.

'Last night, Lucas—Mr Varley,' said Catherine, to Keely's mind going a shade pink, 'asked me to marry him.'

'L . . . Mr Var . . .' Keely had had no idea what it was her mother had come to London specially to tell her, but never would she have guessed that it was this! Utterly staggered, she stared and just stared. And it was not until she came a little way from her shock to note that Catherine was looking more than a shade apprehensive, that she was able to find her voice to ask, 'What—what was your answer?'

'I said—yes.' Keely was still struggling with shock, but when Catherine added, a note of apprehension mingling with the apprehensive look, 'Do you mind?' that shock was to depart, and leave room only for pleasure.

'Mind!' she replied. 'I'm thrilled for you.'

It was true too. Even if this was the first she had heard that there had been something growing between her mother and Lucas Varley, as Catherine's apprehension gave way to show her inner happiness, Keely was delighted.

It was touch and go then that had not a waiter come

to serve them, as the excitement that had been in her mother's voice surfaced again, Keely would not have left her chair to give her a big hug.

But the impulse passed with the disappearance of the waiter, so, both of them grinning happily, Catherine was saying how since she had never visited Inchbrook she must rectify that, and come and meet Lucas.

'Just say when,' replied Keely, hardly able to wait to meet the man who was responsible for putting this never-before-seen glow into her mother's eyes.

'Lucas suggests this weekend. He'd like us to have a celebratory dinner tomorrow night. Tarrant is coming home for the weekend as he usually does, so Lucas thought you might like to stay and that it would be a nice family get-together.'

Keely's smile beamed across the table. 'I'll be there first thing tomorrow,' she said. 'I can't wait to meet Mr Varley.' Her mind was already on what dress to take with her for this special occasion dinner, when, mentally discarding one dress, she remembered that that had been the one she was going to wear tomorrow night for her date with Gerald. 'Oh . . .!' she exclaimed, having forgotten all about him.

'Problem?'

'No, not really,' answered Keely, her smile going into hiding as she wondered if Gerald would ever speak to her again—though surely he would understand? 'Gerald,' she said, having no need to say who Gerald was since she had told Catherine all about him, 'has managed to get some rarer-than-grass-in-the-desert tickets for the theatre tomorrow night. In a weak moment, I said I'd go with him.' Her smile came out again. 'But I'm sure he'll understand when I tell him . . .'

'No, don't cancel!' Catherine butted in abruptly, causing Keely to look at her, startled. 'It would be a shame to disappoint him,' she said more slowly. 'Particularly if the tickets have been so difficult to obtain. Besides . . .' she broke off, for the first time a trace of worry wrinkling her brow.

'Besides—what?' prompted Keely, not prepared to leave it there. Nothing should be allowed to worry her mother at what should be such a happy time for her. These past two years hadn't been easy for her, nor, given her father's irascible temperament, had the years before that, she suspected.

'It's—nothing,' Catherine hedged.

But Keely wasn't having that. 'So tell me, then we can have a laugh about it.'

'I'm just being silly,' Catherine replied—but had to confess when her daughter wouldn't let it go, 'It was Lucas's idea that we should all be together under the one roof this weekend. But—well,' and at the look from Keely that said they had never had any secrets, 'Well, to tell you the truth, Keely, I'm not sure that it wouldn't be better for his son to get used to the idea a little first before the Macfarlanes get their feet firmly established under the table—Lucas said he'd leave it till tomorrow to give Tarrant the good news.'

Amazed, Keely stared. 'You're saying that you think Tarrant might not see what his father has to tell him as good news? You think his son might *object*?' she exclaimed.

'No, not really,' said Catherine quickly. 'But . . .'

To Keely's thinking as she made her way back to the office, whatever her parent had said, there must be a definite doubt in her mind that Tarrant Varley might object, and very strongly, to her marrying his father.

She had never met either Varley, nor was she going to this weekend. That empathy she had with her mother made her see that Catherine had enough to cope with this weekend without having any added problems which could crop up if, faint though she was making out Tarrant Varley's objections might be, he came out strongly against the marriage. Her mother knew her well. That being so, she knew that if Lucas Varley didn't sort his son out for his nerve, then she wasn't the type of daughter who would let anyone ride rough-shod over her mother.

But, in having agreed for the sake of her mother's peace of mind to leave meeting Lucas until the following weekend, Keely still worried constantly about her for most of that weekend when Tarrant Varley would be paying his usual visit to his home.

The show Gerald took her to was as good as its reputation, and at any other time she would have enjoyed it immensely. But there were not many minutes during the entire performance when her mind was free from the thought—had Tarrant Varley been told yet, and was he as pleased as she had been?

Sunday proved to be one of those Sundays that stretched out endlessly. Desperately wanting to get on the phone to Inchbrook, knowing that she would know straight away from her mother's voice how things had gone, Keely restrained the urge.

From what she could remember of previous conversations with her mother, Tarrant Varley had a small flat in London, but still regarded Inchbrook as his home and returned there most weekends, leaving just after dinner on Sunday evening.

Better, she thought, to ring after he had left. If things had gone badly, then her mother would be able to talk more freely after he had departed.

At half past nine, whether Lucas Varley's son had left for his *pied-à-terre* or not, Keely could wait no longer.

'It's me,' she said brightly, when her mother answered the phone.

'Hello, Keely,' Catherine answered, the same forced bright note being bounced back, and not fooling Keely for a minute. 'How nice of you to ring.'

Nice of her to ring! To her mind Keely was for ever on the phone to her. 'How are things?' she asked. 'How did the dinner go on Saturday?'

'Fine—fine,' replied Catherine. But it was obvious to

her daughter that things had gone far from well—or why else didn't she want to talk about it? Her question of, 'How was the theatre?' told Keely far more than her mother suspected.

'Terrific!' she enthused, plucking out of thin air what she could remember so her mother would not know that she had seen straight through her 'Fine—fine.'

Having put down the phone, Keely then spent a few minutes in thought. No mention had been made of her proposed visit to Inchbrook next weekend. But in any case, she couldn't wait that long to find out what had gone on. And since it was obvious that her mother was going to tell her nothing over the telephone, there seemed to be only one answer. The next time Keely picked up the phone she dialled a different number.

'It's Keely,' she told Gerald when after a long wait the phone was eventually answered. 'I'm sorry to disturb you at this time of night.'

'I wasn't in bed,' he replied, a warmth in his voice coming over the wires, as he added, 'but you can disturb me any time, Keely.'

'Actually, Gerald,' she said, managing to keep her voice light, 'I wondered if you could do without me tomorrow?'

'Where are you going?' was his prompt possessive answer, the warmth leaving just as promptly.

'Not for an interview for another job,' she said quickly, wondering if another job might be the answer to her 'What should she do about Gerald' problem, though she liked her work, and it paid well. 'The thing is,' she invented, 'there are still some bits and pieces outstanding to do with my father's estate. I . . .'

'It takes an age to clear everything up, doesn't it?' he agreed, going on to tell her how when his father had died he had still been signing documents years afterwards.

'That's why I need the day off,' Keely got in quickly, glad of his unconscious help. 'Mother has something I have to sign, and since it appears fairly urgent—and she just can't have another day off so soon,' she added at speed, 'I said that I'd go down to the Varley place tomorrow.'

With Gerald's, 'I'll have to wait until Tuesday to see you, then,' ringing in her ears, Keely put down the phone, her mind back with her mother.

The tall, slim, smartly dressed girl who got off the train the following morning, and asked the taxi driver to take her to Inchbrook, had the light of battle in her eyes. The hours between her saying goodbye to her boss on the phone and to her leaving her flat had seen her blood temperature soaring.

That she looked cool, calm and controlled as the taxi sped towards its destination was only brought about by Keely instilling in herself that she must listen first, and fire afterwards. For in those hours of thinking every which way on what had taken place since Tarrant Varley had been acquainted with the news that he was to have a stepmother, she had become more and more convinced that those doubts her mother had that he might have some objection to raise had been proved correct. And nobody slighted her mother—not while she was around they didn't!

How many miles it was to Inchbrook from the station, Keely didn't know. But the ride seemed to go on for ever. Though that could, she realised, be because she was so anxious to get there. But the taxi had long since left the built-up area and was in green belt country when the driver took a turn which then led up to a winding drive, at the top of which was a tall stately house. Keely had arrived at Inchbrook.

With no intention of going round to the back of the impressive building, she paid off the taxi driver and went up to the stout oak front door, to ring the bell and chance who answered.

As soon as she saw him she knew that the tall lean man with his crop of white hair was Lucas Varley. And the fact that he had no objection to answering his own front door when she knew from her mother that he had day staff apart from his live-in housekeeper made her warm to him.

'Hello,' she said, and could not hold back on a smile for the twinkly-eyed man who was waiting for her to state her business, 'I'm Keely Macfarlane.'

His smile was all she could wish for. It told her that whatever objection his son had had to raise, her mother was still a favourite person, and her daughter more than welcome.

'Come in, come in,' he beamed at her, his hand coming out straight away to shake hands. 'I'm Lucas Varley. Catherine didn't tell me you were coming. But then she's full of delightful little surprises.'

What a lovely man he is, she couldn't help thinking, some of the tight anger in her disappearing at her welcome, hope in her that she had worked herself up over nothing as she crossed the threshold.

'Your mother's in the kitchen,' Lucas Varley told her as he led her along a wide hall and kitchenwards. 'She's still insisting on doing every bit of cooking herself, although I've told her that we'll get someone else in to do it.'

'She's a good cook,' said Keely.

'None better,' he agreed, opening a door at the far end of the hall, exclaiming with the eagerness of one who liked to do some surprising himself to the woman coring apples over by the sink, 'Didn't know I was a magician, did you, Catherine?'

'Keely!' exclaimed Catherine, spinning round.

Keely saw the smile on her mother's face, instant for Lucas, instant for her. But sadly, she also saw that that bubbling inner happiness that had been in her as recently as last Friday was no longer there. Fair enough, she thought, as she went over to give Catherine a hug and a kiss, everyone came down to earth some time, but—so soon!

'I couldn't wait until the weekend to meet Mr

Varley,' she explained, her keen glance going from one to the other. 'Do you mind?'

'Not if you exchange that Mr Varley for calling me Lucas,' said her prospective stepfather with the charm she saw must have bowled her mother over. Then he told Catherine to leave whatever she was doing, that they could have bread and dripping for lunch as far as he was concerned, but that the kitchen was no place to entertain Keely.

Shepherding them to the drawing room, Lucas stopped a vacuum-cleaner-carrying young woman who was coming down the stairs, to ask her if she had a minute to make some coffee.

'Certainly, Mr Varley,' she replied, and with a willing smile to Catherine, she scooted off to the kitchen they had just left.

Talk in the drawing room was general until the coffee arrived. Then with a steady look at her daughter, Catherine asked pointedly how she had managed to get the day off.

'I've a lot of time due to me, actually,' Keely answered lightly, turning to explain to Lucas how she had started to work for Gerald Cullen last May, but how since his previous secretary had left at short notice, things had been in rather a muddle, and what with that and learning her new job, she hadn't found time to use all her holiday allowance.

'But you'll take all your holiday allowance this year,' he suggested. 'I insist that you come and spend some time at Inchbrook with Catherine and me, so that I can get to know you.'

Keely smiled her acceptance, but saw that her mother did not enthuse over his suggestion, nor did she in any way look as happy about it as she would have done last Friday. But to cover what could have been an uncomfortable pause, Keely jumped in to mention that the firm she worked for did some work occasionally for Varley Industries.

'That's right,' Lucas agreed. 'Cullen's have come on well since we first started dealing with them. Cullen himself must be on his way to being a millionaire by now.'

'He says that that's what the taxman thinks.'

'Don't we all,' said Lucas, setting his empty coffee cup down on the tray and getting to his feet. 'I expect you'll want to have a bit of a chat, so I'll leave you to it and see what's to do in my workshop. I'll see you at lunch,' he smiled. Then, turning to Catherine, 'Don't forget to tell Keely our arrangements, my dear.'

Keely waited only until the door had closed. 'Arrangements?' she queried.

'Lucas can't see any reason for us to wait—he wants us to be married within a month.'

Keely's impression of Lucas was that he was a man who seldom did not get what he went after. His charm alone, without that determined chin, would see him halfway to ensuring that, she thought.

'But you want to wait a while?' she asked, knowing it for the truth without her mother hesitating to meet her eyes.

'Why have you come, Keely?' she enquired, not answering the question.

'You're saying I'm not welcome?'

'Oh, love, never that, but . . .'

She and her mother had never gone in for pussyfooting round an issue, to Keely's mind, and now did not seem the time to start. 'What happened when Lucas told his son?' she asked point-blank. She was to see sadness in Catherine's eyes as, shaking her head, she replied:

'Don't ask.'

'But I am asking,' she insisted. 'As far as Mr Varley—Lucas—is concerned, everything between you is the same as you told me it was on Friday. What's happened in the meantime that has you wanting to wait a while before you marry him? It's got something to do with Tarrant Varley's reaction, I know damn well it has!'

Normally, she would have earned herself a mild reproof for her language. But as Catherine raised her sad eyes to that look on her daughter's face that said she was going to sit there all week if need be, but that she was not moving until she had heard how Tarrant Varley had received the news, that reproof was never heard.

But as, piece by piece, Keely got everything out of her, so as her anger rocketed, Keely's mind found words that made the 'damn' she had used sound tepid in comparison.

Enraged by what her mother had imparted, scarcely able to believe her hearing at first, when everything that there was to hear had been said, she knew there was just no way that she could sit at Lucas Varley's table for lunch and not express what she thought of his diabolical son.

How she managed to invent suddenly remembering some extremely urgent papers her boss wanted to take to a meeting that afternoon, but would not be able to get because she had the key to the cabinet as an excuse for not stopping to lunch, she did not know.

But with Lucas at the wheel as they drove her to the station, only just did Keely manage to keep a lid on her fury. She even managed to say a polite goodbye to Lucas as though nothing had happened. But as she sat in the train going over everything her mother had told her, Keely was boiling over with rage.

Apparently Tarrant Varley had behaved himself quite well over dinner, after which, his father thinking his son was being tactful, he had gone off out somewhere.

'But he wasn't being tactful?' she had asked.

'No, I'm sure he left us alone because he was too furious at the news to be able to contain his anger if he had to be in the same room with me any longer.'

'Who the hell ...' Keely had started to rage, but bottled down that first spurt of rocketing anger as she saw she might well put her mother off telling the whole of it if she asked who the hell did he think he was. 'What you're really saying,' she went on, choking down her fury and trying desperately hard to be fair, 'is that without him saying a word, you received a general impression that—like some children do—Tarrant Varley didn't take very kindly to being presented with a future stepmother?'

'Tarrant Varley, apart from the fact that he's thirty-six and has had sole responsibility for the running of Varley Industries since his father retired two years ago, is a fully grown man,' Catherine explained, to show that there was nothing of the child about him. 'And his mother has been dead this past twenty years,' she added tiredly. 'No, it isn't that I'm taking his mother's place that's infuriating him, I'm sure of that. Not that I would aim to take her place anyway,' she said proudly.

'Then what?' she had persisted, in a maze as to know why the fact of Lucas marrying again should have his son and heir unable to stay in the same room with his father's intended bride longer than he had to. 'Why doesn't he want his father to marry you? What reason ...'

'Because ...' Suddenly, as she watched, so her mother seemed to crumple. The next second Keely was out of her chair and going to her. 'Because,' Catherine went on, 'I was—his father's housekeeper, I think.'

'You think! B-because ... My God!' Keely stuttered. And, unable to believe it, 'You've made a mistake. People aren't that snobby any more ...' Catherine shaking her head had her breaking off.

'No, I haven't, Keely. I wish I had,' she said. And if Keely had found what she had heard so far mind-blowing, then she was to stare at her mother in utter stupefaction, not believing her ears when she heard her add, 'He came into the kitchen while I was preparing breakfast yesterday morning and . . . and tried to . . . to buy me off.'

Speechlessly Keely looked at the crumpled figure of her proud mother sitting crushed to have revealed what she had had to reveal.

'He did *what*!' Still not believing she had heard correctly, she stared thunderstruck.

'He'd—actually got a cheque all ready written out—a very substantial cheque, I must say,' confirmed Catherine as she swallowed unhappily. 'He—he suggested that his cheque might make my leaving—less painful.'

'Leaving?' Keely was still incredulous. But she was then being assaulted by so many outraged feelings all at once that she was having to fight hard to hold them down; to hold down too the most pulling impulse of all—that of going in search of Lucas Varley wherever his workshop might be, and telling him exactly what her mother had told her. For it was obvious to her, from Lucas's greeting of her, his manner in general, without what she knew of her mother's character, that she had not told him what a rat he had got for a son.

Stamping down hard on all impulses, Keely had only one question to ask from all she had heard.

'Tell me, darling,' she said, with all the control she could muster, 'do you love Lucas?'

'Yes,' Catherine answered without hesitation. 'I know I haven't known him long. But seeing him every day this last three months, I . . .'

'Then you're going to marry him in a month's time as he has asked,' said Keely firmly. 'And this—Tarrant creature—can go to the devil!'

Stepping out of the train when she reached London, Keely was oblivious to any of the hustle and bustle around her. She had been more furious than she had ever been in her life at what her mother had told her. And as she relived every word in the train just now, thinking of the utter gall of that snobby individual who had *dared* to try and buy her mother off, that fury had magnified the more she thought of the outrageous way he had insulted her wonderful parent.

Every Londoner knew where Varley Industries was. Keely did not even bother to give the address as she stepped into a taxi and said shortly, 'The Varley Industries Building.'

My God, she thought as the taxi moved off, if Tarrant Varley thought he could so degradingly insult her mother and then walk away without hearing another word about it—did he have another think coming!

CHAPTER TWO

By the time the taxi had dropped her off at the Varley Industries Building, having stewed with indignation throughout her train journey, Keely's storming rage had reached a fine peak. So that by the time she had blatantly lied her way past reception and was about to go through the door where she had gleaned she would find Tarrant Varley's secretary, and ultimately him, she was ready to explode from seething fury.

To go in and find his secretary standing right in front of another door, the door she was ready to blaze straight through, the notepad in her hand indicating that she had just left him, halted Keely. She had entered the office without stopping to knock, but she saw that short of pushing the secretary, who hadn't moved out of her way, she was going to have to say something in answer to that look of enquiry.

Swallowing some of her ire—needs must if this secretary was as protective of her boss's time as she was of Gerald's—Keely sought for and found just the right breezy note to ask:

'Is Tarrant free at the moment?'

'Er——' murmured the pretty secretary, thrown for a brief moment, 'he's not expecting you, is he?'

'Oh no,' said Keely blithely, inwardly fuming. Keely Macfarlane was the last person Tarrant Varley was expecting to see at his office, but he *was* going to see her even if she did have to resort to pushing the secretary out of the way to achieve that end. 'I just happened to be passing and only just remembered in time what Tarrant had threatened to do to me if I ever came this close and didn't look in.'

She was glad to see that the secretary's eyes were now

taken up with assessing the good quality of the sage green two-piece she had thought to put on to go down to Inchbrook that morning. With her eyes on the fine wool skirt and hip-length three-quarter-sleeve jumper top, and its contrasting green neck scarf, her attention was away from the green eyes which Keely thought must surely be revealing that inside she was hopping mad.

'Actually,' she said, lowering her voice confidingly, knowing very well that this was the first the secretary had heard of it since Tarrant Varley was still hoping it wasn't going to happen, 'I'm soon to be Tarrant's stepsister.'

The other girl's surprise was all the confirmation she needed to know that the rat in there had not breathed a word to a soul about his father being about to remarry.

'Mr Varley senior is . . .!' she started to exclaim.

'That's right,' said Keely, getting practised now in the art of smiling with her mouth alone. 'Tarrant's father and my mother are to be married in four weeks' time.'

Though she dearly wanted to charge in behind her, as with a muttered, 'Excuse me one moment,' the secretary turned about and went through the door, closing it behind her, pride came to check Keely. When she told that swine in there what she thought of him, since her mother's name would probably come into it, for her sake it had to be kept private.

The secretary was not long. But instead of saying that Mr Varley had given instructions for her to be escorted off the premises, to Keely's surprise, she smiled as she said:

'Mr Varley will see you now if you'd care to go in.'

Surprise kept her motionless for all of one second. Then she was forgetting to return the secretary's smile, and the anger that had been held down with difficulty was once more come to the surface.

In a few rapid strides she had crossed the pale grey carpeting, and was through the door, and closing it on the secretary with a determined click. Then she was face to face with the tall, strongly built man who stood behind his desk, and who had had the unspeakable nerve to treat her mother the way he had.

'So you're what a high-and-mighty rat looks like,' she flew in for openers, her green eyes sparking, her usually pale creamy complexion for once slightly flushed from the heat of her fury. 'I've . . .' was as far as she got.

'Your mother said you were beautiful,' interrupted the blond-haired, hard-grey-eyed individual who stood looking her over. 'In that respect, at least, she wasn't lying.'

'My mother never tells lies,' Keely defended hotly, his remark to her looks barely registering as she heard only the non-too-subtle implication that he thought her mother a liar in all other respects. 'But you wouldn't know that, would you? You haven't bothered to find out the first thing about her sweet character. All you can see is that a mere housekeeper is likely to become your stepmother, and that,' she charged on, 'as far as you in your snobby "My God, what will the neighbours say" world,' she was too overheated to remember that from what she had seen, Inchbrook did not appear to have any neighbours near, 'is so unthinkable to you that . . .'

'Have you finished?' Bluntly he sliced through her tirade, his eyes going from hard to become granite chips of rock.

'I haven't even started yet,' Keely raged on, impervious to the impatience in the man, impervious to the fact that he was growing to look more hostile by the second—not that he had been at all welcoming before.

'You've said all you're going to say,' she found herself contradicted cuttingly.

'Huh!' she scorned angrily, ignoring his meaningful look to the door. 'You might think you can trample all over people like me and my mother, but I'm here to tell you differently. I'm here to tell you that my mother *is* going to marry your father. I hope,' she added, reading his thoughts correctly she was sure, '*over* your dead body, and you can stuff that in your cheque book and cash it!' she tacked on insolently.

'So she told you I'd offered her money, did she?' he asked, his eyes narrowing. 'Quite obviously I didn't offer her enough.'

A red haze was suddenly in front of Keely as his insulting words left him. 'Why, you . . .' she shrieked— but found Tarrant Varley was again slicing through her rage.

'She didn't waste much time in telling you, did she?'

'For your information, Mr Stuck-up Varley, I had to prise that information out of her,' Keely hurled across at him. 'I knew that something was wrong when I telephoned her last night. But it wasn't until I went down to see her this morning that . . .'

She had suspected that Tarrant Varley was not without a temper himself. But she was to witness that he could be furious in an instant. For abruptly he had left his casual stance behind his desk, and had moved to come and fiercely take hold of her arm, his face like a thundercloud, his aversion to a second Macfarlane entering his home obvious, as he demanded:

'You've been down to Inchbrook?'

'What's the matter, Varley?' Keely challenged right back, as she tugged impotently to be free. 'Upset because I didn't use the tradesman's entrance?'

'Don't be ridiculous,' he barked, throwing her arm from him as he glared into her sizzling green eyes. 'I just had not credited that there could be two Macfarlane vultures after the pickings.'

'Vultures?' she echoed, stunned for a second, not believing her ears. Then a fury unlike any other fury took charge of her. It mattered not what he called her, but that he should dare to call her mother a vulture was past standing.

With a crack that, had she been more practised in

dealing such blows, would surely have broken his cheekbone, her hand had streaked through the air and connected. But in the startled silence that followed, where Keely was shattered at her own violence, she saw that Tarrant too seemed stunned by it, because he just stood and stared as if he couldn't believe it.

Then it was that as he took one long-drawn-in breath to give her the impression that he was struggling against all odds not to send her slap stingingly back, Keely saw that she had just about topped anything else she would have found to say. That there was nothing left to say, that that blow, had said it all for her.

Though she was to find, as he continued to struggle for control, and she moved quickly to the door, that she was still angry, with an anger that was insisting on her having one parting shot.

'Talking of vultures,' she tossed at him, 'you might consider this before the wedding takes place,' and, ready then to get out of there smartish if he moved just one step, 'Whereas, while all I'm interested in is my parent's happiness—can you say the same?' His control straining as his look became more threatening—it was her cue to start turning the door handle. 'Is it Lucas's happiness you're interested in?' she asked, her eye judging the distance between them as deliberately she used his father's first name, not missing that it hadn't helped Tarrant Varley in his search for self-control, 'or is it that you're more interested in protecting your inheritance from the preying Macfarlanes than you are in his happiness?'

Moving like lightning, she just made it through the door as he got to it. 'Goodbye,' she bade the secretary brightly, still on the move, aware that her future stepbrother was staring after her in the doorway, 'I think Mr Varley could do with a couple of aspirins!'

It was on a Saturday morning four weeks later that Keely got out of bed to take a more than usual interest in the weather. Today was her mother's wedding day. She took a glance out of her flat window to see that April was behaving itself, showers looking unlikely from a sky that was brilliantly blue.

After a quick bath she put on her new pale pink silk dress bought especially for the occasion, hoping that the rest of the day would continue as sunnily as it had started—in more ways than one.

It had been her mother's wish that she stay at Inchbrook over Friday night, but as dearly as she would have liked to have done nothing better, Keely suspected that Lucas had asked his son to do the self-same thing, and she had made some excuse.

She was in no hurry to renew her acquaintance with Tarrant Varley. It was for that reason, knowing he went home most weekends, that she had cried off the weekend visit to Inchbrook which she had previously agreed to.

All she hoped was that Tarrant Varley behaved himself today. Without a doubt he had not missed a weekend at Inchbrook since his father had told him of his marriage plans. Not that she knew that definitely, because when speaking on the phone to her mother, knowing she would not be able to keep back something short and pithy if his name came up, she had held back from asking anything about him. Just as, for the first time ever, she had held back from telling her mother about something—that something that she had gone to his office and had landed him a beauty, and had just got out before he had returned the compliment.

Catherine had not mentioned him either. And Keely could only glean from that that her mother was keeping to her usual code which said if she couldn't say anything good about someone, then she wouldn't say anything at all.

As she had the one and only other time she had visited Inchbrook, Keely took a taxi from the station that Saturday. Catherine had said Lucas would send a car to meet her train, but, not wanting to be under the smallest obligation to Tarrant Varley if his father asked him to pick her up, she had invented train times often being re-scheduled on Saturdays, and said she was not sure at what time she would arrive. Though knowing what she did about her soon-to-be-stepbrother, had he so been delegated, she wouldn't have put it past him to drive around for an hour and then go back and say that she hadn't been on the train—Keely was taking no chances.

With everything telling her that Tarrant Varley was going to spoil this day for her mother if he could, only she was not going to let him, Keely paid off the taxi driver as the village clock struck the half hour. That made it half past twelve, she thought, standing in front of the stately house which would soon see her mother as mistress. She was in ample time for the three o'clock ceremony as she had promised.

Wondering, as she had before, who would open the door to her, Keely kept a smile from her face just in case it was that swine Tarrant Varley.

But her smile needed no prompting when the door opened and she saw her mother standing there. 'Hello, darling,' said Keely, and hugged the slim tense body to her, tears threatening to choke her as the thought came that Catherine had not had it too easy, but now, pray God, life was going to be better for her.

'You're looking as pretty as a picture,' said Catherine, standing back at last and surveying her daughter.

'And so are you,' replied Keely, guessing that she was nervous, though hopeful that it was only bridal nerves, and did not stem from anything the disgruntled son of the house had said to her.

'I haven't changed yet!'

'That doesn't stop you from looking pretty whatever you're wearing,' Keely piled it on.

'Oh, love, it's so good to see you,' said her mother,

her nerves definitely showing, Keely thought, as she forbore to ask if Lucas's son had been putting his crabby oar in. 'Come into the drawing room,' said Catherine, collecting herself. 'I'll introduce you to Tarrant.'

'Where's Lucas?' asked Keely, unsure that Tarrant wouldn't give away the fact that they had already met—even if that introduction had been totally without civilities—though guessing that he would not refer to that meeting if his father were present.

'They're both in the drawing room. There's a cold lunch laid in the breakfast room if you're hungry,' Catherine told her as they went. 'And a buffet meal is ready in the dining room for when we come back from the church.'

'I think I'll wait until then,' murmured Keely as she followed her into the drawing room.

Lucas got to his feet, as spritely as any young man as they entered. But Keely, her eyes flicking straight to the man she had once had the enormous pleasure of striking, saw that it was only reluctant good manners that had him idly shifting himself.

'Keely!' said Lucas, looking as happy as he should be looking, she thought, as he bent to kiss the cheek of the young woman who would soon be his stepdaughter. Keely looking over his shoulder, met full on the granite-hard eyes which she had once seen furious. Then Lucas was letting go of her, and turning to say, 'This is my son Tarrant. Tarrant—Keely.'

'How nice to meet you,' smiled Keely, extending her hand as all along she had promised herself she would, no matter what feelings went on inside her. Today was her mother's day, and nothing, she vowed, was going to spoil it.

'Keely,' he acknowledged, making no attempt to smile, but taking the hand that had struck him in a firm grasp, his eyes hard on hers as his left hand came up to the side of his face to indicate that he had not forgotten that slap, nor would he in a hurry.

The moment he let go her hand she turned her back on him, her ears picking up the fact that her mother was telling Lucas that she was going to go up to change.

It was early yet for her to change into her wedding outfit, Keely thought, knocking yet another nail in the coffin of her hate for Tarrant Varley that her mother was in a highly nervous state because he was there.

'I'll come with you, shall I?' she asked warmly, and knew she was not mistaken about her mother's nerves when she threw her a grateful look.

The rooms Catherine took her to were large and well furnished. And having gone from the private sitting room, Keely saw that the bedroom was very similar to the one which had been her mother's before their old home had been sold. Though having seen that her accommodation while working for Lucas was as comfortable as she could wish, Keely was more interested in trying to help her with her nerves.

All brides must be nervous on their wedding day, she mused, whatever their age. But with instinct sharp in her, Keely knew that the presence of Tarrant Varley after the despicable way he had offered her money to leave had no small part to play in the way her mother was feeling.

'Are Tarrant and I the only relatives attending the wedding?' she asked, talking purely for the sake of talking. Most of the relatives on the Macfarlane side were getting on in years and were disinclined to travel. And if Aunt Shelagh, her mother's sister, was to be there, then Catherine would have told her before this.

'Relatives are few on Lucas's side,' Catherine answered, taking fresh underwear from her chest of drawers and setting it out on the bed ready for when she had had her bath. 'For the most part they're far-flung cousins anyway.'

'You didn't ask Aunt Shelagh to come?'

'I did, actually,' Catherine smiled, and her look softened as she added. 'When Lucas knew I had a sister I was very fond of, he insisted that she should be here today.'

'But you thought, since Lucas won't be having any other of his kin here, that you wouldn't invite her?'

To Keely's relief, Catherine was starting to lose that nervous look. 'I said Lucas had insisted,' she reminded her. 'He's a very determined man once he makes his mind up.'

Keely remembered his determined chin, that chin that had had her thinking that once he put his mind to it, it was seldom he did not get his way. She had seen that same determined chin elsewhere, she was to recall, as her mother went on opening drawers. And she had no difficulty in remembering where. But whereas she had thought it was seldom that Lucas Varley did not get what he went after, the granite-hard eyes that went with the other Varley who had inherited that same chin, made her think that Tarrant Varley *always* got what he went after.

'So Aunt Shelagh will be here!' she took up somewhat belatedly, but a happy smile coming to play about her mouth, because, his cheque book being just so much printed paper, this was one time when Tarrant Varley had not got what he wanted.

Her mother shaking her head told her that she had got it wrong. 'I heard from her yesterday,' she said. 'Apparently Jeanette is newly pregnant and is having a dreadful time.'

'Oh no!' cried Keely, knowing immediately that the Butterworth Factor had been inherited by her cousin Jeanette, Aunt Shelagh's daughter.

'I'm afraid so,' Catherine replied. 'That's why your aunt can't come. With Jeanette's husband travelling all over the country with his job—he's away at the moment—Shelagh is staying with Jeanette for a while,

and doesn't feel like leaving her until he gets back. So,'
she ended, 'it'll be just the four of us.'

Keely noticed that her mother was starting to look a
shade nervy again as those words fell from her lips.

'What you need is a nice relaxing bath,' she said, and,
firmly taking charge, 'I'll go and run it for you.'

The service in the small village church was
everything, and more, that Keely could have hoped.
Misty-eyed, she forgot about the tall immaculately
suited man with his eyes on the two people exchanging
their vows, room only there for her to see, and feel an
inner glow, at the way Lucas looked at her mother as he
turned to take her as his wife. It was there, the look she
had wanted to see, that look that said he cared deeply
for her.

That her mother, looking lovely dressed all in blue
with blue shoes, and a matching blue hat, seemed to
have forgotten everything too, except the man she
was being married to, made it all so much more
perfect.

With no photographer there, Keely was glad she had
thought to slip her camera into her bag. But with a snap
of the happy couple safely on film, she had to think
quickly for an answer when Lucas held out his hand for
her camera and said:

'Let me take one of you with Tarrant.'

That Tarrant chose to pretend he had not heard his
father, and had moved off to open the door of his
father's car, suited her just fine. 'It's your day,' she
grinned. 'Tarrant and I can have our picture taken
together some other time.'

Because they had gone to the church in two separate
cars, Keely, when she would by far have preferred to
walk back to the house, for her mother's sake
swallowed her pride, and stepped once more into
Tarrant's Ferrari.

Though hardly had she sat down and closed the door
before he was driving off. Ignorant swine! she thought,

seat-belt law or no seat-belt law, halfway to the house before she had got it fixed into position.

She would have preferred too that they dawdled back so as to give the newlyweds the chance of more than just a few minutes together. But no such thought had occurred to Tarrant. And that he was a sore loser was abundantly plain, for not so much as a grunt came her way in the half-mile journey back to the house.

'Champagne,' greeted Lucas, when, to her surprise Tarrant remembered his manners sufficiently to let her go into the house before him.

But whether he drank any of the champagne that had been handed to him, she neither knew nor cared; her mother could well do without any toast from him. That he was not hungry when in high spirits Lucas came to urge them to the dining room, was all right by her too. She could well do without that feeling of his eyes glaring at her back.

Though having been of the opinion that the day was going exceedingly well for the only two people who mattered, Keely, having just demolished a couple of delicately thin smoked salmon sandwiches, was to stare in amazement when for one of the brief times Lucas was away from her mother's side, Catherine, offering her another sandwich, asked her to stay at Inchbrook that night.

'Stay here—tonight?' she exclaimed, knowing full well that Lucas and Catherine had decided on a cruise later and were not going away. Then her lips started to twitch. And she just could not resist the teasing comment, 'I really think I should have had a mother-and-daughter talk with you—darling, this is your honeymoon!'

'I know,' said Catherine, trying to smile, but not succeeding very well.

'You won't want your daughter around at dinner,' Keely went on, still trying to get a natural smile out of her mother. 'Why, Lucas will want you to himself once Tarrant and I have gone . . .'

'Tarrant isn't going,' Catherine interrupted, biting her lip.

'Tarrant isn't . . .!' Astonishment prevented her finishing.

'He's staying for the weekend.'

'He's *what*!' Keely exclaimed, trying to recover from her appalled astonishment, but finding it difficult.

'Well, it is his home,' said Catherine, trying hard to be fair.

Lucas came in at that point, and they both smiled at him. But as Keely made play of deciding whether she wanted trifle or fruit salad, suddenly having no appetite for either, her thoughts were going fast and furious.

The unspeakable swine! she was inwardly raging. While his father had wanted to employ another housekeeper to take her mother's place, that devil was determined to see her mother as a housekeeper and not as now she was, his father's wife. Mentally calling Tarrant Varley all the names she could put her tongue to, Keely saw clearly that her dear mother would never be accepted by him in her new position—that of mistress of Inchbrook. Why, he'd probably expect her to wait on him hand and foot still. Expect her, since they did not employ weekend staff at Inchbrook, to tidy his room and make his bed for him tomorrow—on her honeymoon too!

Suddenly Keely's anger was too much to be borne quietly.

'I can recommend the fruit salad,' said Lucas, one arm about her mother's shoulders as he came over with her to help Keely with what appeared to be a difficult choice, she had dithered so long.

'I've just decided that if I eat another mouthful, I shall burst at the seams,' she replied with a light laugh. 'I'll leave you to it,' she smiled, and casually, her look belying her inner fury, she strolled from the dining room.

But there was nothing ambling about the way she went charging into the drawing room where Tarrant, his long legs stretched out in front of him, was lounging on the settee.

'Haven't you any more tact?' she hissed, too furious to come to the point gradually.

Arrogantly, his face as unsmiling as hers, Tarrant Varley let his eyes travel up from the toes of her shoes, past her shapely legs and shapely hips, lingered a moment at her bustline covered in its pretty pink, then on to her pink-tinged with anger, flawless complexion.

'Plenty—when it's needed,' he drawled idly, making no attempt to get to his feet.

'Well, it's needed now!' she snapped. 'If you have so much as an atom of the tact you claim to possess, you will change your mind about staying at Inchbrook tonight!'

He did not like it, she saw, that she was as good as ordering him from his own home. But he didn't bite, his contemptuously careless manner staying with him, as, with no apology whatsoever, he replied:

'You'll forgive me, I'm sure, for wanting to be around when the scales fall from my father's eyes.' And while Keely looked as though she was going to blow a fuse, and indeed had a desperate struggle not to again send her right hand aiming for his cheekbone, softly, his eyes on the twin spots of colour, one either side of her face, he added, 'It had crossed my mind to extend my weekend here.' And while she was gasping at that, 'In fact, I might well hang around Inchbrook for the whole of next week.'

'You swine!' she hissed. 'You cynical, devilish swine! You don't give a damn how much injury you add to the insult you served my mother, do you? Not content with trying to make her look small by trying to buy her off, you're out to ruin this marriage if you can before it gets started!'

'I thought it was only one phoney I was dealing with. But now,' he mocked, 'by all appearances, I have two to deal with.'

'What do you mean by that?' she flared, the need to take a swing at him starting to get out of hand.

'I thought, when your mother refused my offer, that she was after bigger pickings. But now, since you've joined the fray with this display of outraged indignation, I can see that you're both in this together.'

'My God!' stunned at the way his mind worked, Keely was speechless to find a reply, her brain numbed that anyone should think what he thought, let alone say it!

'My sentiments exactly,' he said harshly, moving from his lounging attitude on the settee quickly on to his feet, to stand towering over her, his expression grim as he grated, 'By the time I'm through with the pair of you, I have no doubt it will have cost me far more than I've forked out to get rid of the eye-to-the-main-chance housekeepers I've had to buy off in the past!'

As her brain came alive again, fresh shock assaulted her, and had the effect of rapidly cooling her fury as she stared at him, trying to make sense of what he had just said.

'You've—you've paid off housekeepers in the past?'

'Two within the last five years,' he told her without shame.

'You mean,' she asked, sure she had seen a look of love in Lucas's eyes for her mother, but fear coming from what his son was saying, that Lucas was ficklehearted, 'You mean that my mother—is not the— the first of his housekeepers your father has asked to be his wife?'

'It didn't get that far,' he replied, to her relief. 'The others were less subtle than your mother—I saw the way the wind was blowing before my father was aware that their greedy, pleasing little attentions were only the start.'

'So, regardless of what your father's feelings were for those other women, whether he could have cared for them or whether they left him cold,' she retorted angrily, 'you stepped in with your infamous cheque book and waited to see what the next housekeeper was going to turn out like!'

Looking down his straight nose at her, Tarrant Varley did not deign to answer. But she had her answer all right. Stuck-up, toffee-nosed, no doubt educated at Eton—though that could be maligning some of the charming men who had got their education at that establishment—he had no fancy to have anyone know that his father had married a one-time housekeeper.

'So you've a down on housekeepers,' she sneered, giving him her own version of an arrogant look.

'And your mother in particular,' he agreed, her lofty look bouncing right off him.

Seeing she was getting nowhere fast—his mind was firmly made up about her mother, she could see that—Keely decided to take another route to get him to change his mind about staying the next week at Inchbrook.

'Can't you see that your father wants to be alone with my mother—that he loves her?' she asked.

'All the more reason for me to stay,' he replied toughly, to make her more incensed.

From his reply she knew that he meant that, loving Catherine, his father would be even more hurt when she showed herself up in her true colours.

'Very well,' she said, and she meant it as she added tautly, 'if you're staying here Tarrant Varley—then so am I.'

Oh dear, she thought, as the fury she had witnessed in him before shot to the surface, he didn't like that, did he!

'You haven't been invited,' he bit out curtly.

'Correction,' she smiled. 'The mistress of the house invited me not half an hour ago.'

'My God!' he bit out in disgust. 'So now the whole bloody Macfarlane family's moving in!'

'Looks like it, doesn't it?' she answered, refusing to rise at his swearing her family name. 'But then, dear stepbrother,' she added sweetly, 'you should know that where you see one vulture, you'll always see two.' And, unable to sustain her sweet tone, bluntly she told him, 'If you're staying here all next week, then that makes two of us.'

Her hand by then had stopped itching to swipe him. In fact she was finding that there was far more satisfaction to be gained from verbally knocking the steps from him than in slapping him.

But if her hand had stopped itching, as almost toe to toe they stood glaring at each other, then Keely had a concrete impression that only by the merest thread of control was Tarrant Varley stopping himself from setting about her.

'What about your job?' he challenged. 'According to your mother, you're the best secretary God ever put breath into. To hear her tell it, Gerald Cullen goes down on his knees every night to give thanks to have you working for him. If you're that efficient, you'd find it unthinkable to leave him in the lurch come Monday.'

Wondering what the dickens her mother had said about her and her work, though without being conceited she knew she was good at her job, Keely determined that Tarrant Varley was not going to have her backing down so easily.

'He can soon borrow one of the other secretaries,' she replied airily. And, finding that sweet note again, 'Besides which, Gerald is a very understanding employer.'

'I'll bet he is,' was the reply, and she didn't miss the suggestion in what he said, as with those words his eyes trailed insultingly down her figure. 'Aiming to be the second Mrs Cullen?' he asked, insolence there as he let her know he was aware that Gerald was divorced and again on the marriage market. But he really made her blood boil when he mocked, 'I should go in to work on Monday girl if I were you. Millionaires are thin on the ground this year, it would be a shame to risk some other secretary having a crack at him, don't you think?'

'For your information,' Keely flared, speaking without thinking first, 'I may have dated Gerald a few times, but I'm not interested in . . .' He cut in before she could add, 'him as a future husband'.

'In his wealth?' he mocked. Keely knew then that she was wasting her breath before she got started.

Not that she had any clear idea, as her mind went on to her mother having to have this monster under the same roof on her honeymoon, how Gerald had crept into the conversation in the first place. But in any case, she was more interested in getting Tarrant to leave than in trying to get through to him that she wasn't the hardhearted gold-digger that he had made up his mind to see her as.

'Look, Tarrant,' she said, her hand itching again that his left eyebrow should ascend to hear her address him as Tarrant, 'can't you see that you're just not wanted here?'

'Now isn't that peculiar,' he answered, as expecting sarcasm, he didn't disappoint her. 'I always thought that Inchbrook was my home.' And for all the world as if he was the most reasonable soul in the world, 'Where would you suggest I go, Miss Macfarlane?'

It was that 'Miss Macfarlane' that did it. The way he was trying to put her in her place and telling her that while she might use his first name, in his opinion, they never would be on friendly enough terms for him to call her by her first name.

'In the absence of the nearest river,' she snapped disagreeably, guessing that he could probably swim like a fish, 'what about your apartment? You've stayed the weekend there before, haven't you?'

For long considering seconds, Tarrant Varley stared at her. But as his eyes then went slowly over her shape, she was to gain a vivid impression that he was remembering what had kept him so occupied in his apartment on those weekends away from Inchbrook.

'So I have,' he drawled at last, and she saw a world of speculation in his eyes. Speculation which was to grow until the moment he appeared to have come to a decision. The speculation was then replaced by a cynical considering expression as he said, 'I'll tell you what I'll do.' And as his eyes stared unblinking into hers, to her immense relief, he told her, 'I'll leave Inchbrook as you've requested—but on one condition.'

'Name it,' she said promptly, never more pleased. And she smiled—it cost her nothing. He smiled too, showing that he had nice even teeth, and Keely felt good too, because, tough struggle though it had been, everything was going to be as she wanted it.

But that was before, still with a smile, a smile she realised later she would have done better than to trust, he calmly dropped:

'I'll return to my flat today—if you, Keely Macfarlane, come and spend the weekend with me.'

Startled out of her briefly happy state, she stared vacantly at him. Surely he could not be meaning what it sounded as though he was meaning! Staggered, she knew for a fact that never in a month of Sundays would he fancy her. Yet . . .

'I'm not quite with . . .' She broke off, suddenly scandalised as his look went to take in the curves of her breasts, and she found that she was indeed right there with him. Yet, her eyes gone enormous, still she struggled for clarification. 'You can't mean . . .' she began, but found even the question was too incredible to ask.

But, if the question had not been put, Keely was to

have all the answer she needed, as witnessing her expression, he scoffed sceptically:

'Oh, my God—such dramatic innocence!'

The door behind her opening made Keely remember as best she could that she had made a mental promise that nothing must be allowed to spoil this day for her mother. Turning from Tarrant, she saw it was her mother who had entered the room and that, if her own nerves were not suddenly starting to play up, Catherine's glance to Tarrant was an anxious one.

'I've just made some tea,' said Catherine pleasantly, even her voice, to her daughter's ears, sounding anxious.

'Lovely,' said Keely enthusiastically as she moved away from Tarrant, her head full of that one unvoiced promise but a promise nonetheless, and how that vow that this day should be perfect for her mother was hanging on one dark and terrible condition.

Going up to her, she reached out and touched her arm affectionately. And all the love she had for Catherine was there in the instant of seeing a trace of anxiety in those dear blue eyes.

Keely flicked her eyes across the room then, seeing Tarrant, but not seeing him, her vision filled with that look in her mother's eyes, that look that had the decision made for her—that vow kept.

'We'll have time for a cup before we leave, won't we, Tarrant?' she asked.

CHAPTER THREE

In no hurry to leave Inchbrook now that she knew that when she departed Tarrant Varley would be leaving too, Keely tried to delay that departure for as long as possible.

Over cups of tea, served in the most delicate china teacups, she chattered brightly away about how kind it was of Tarrant to offer her a lift back to her flat. That he did not contradict her to tell her mother and her new stepfather that it was to his flat he was taking her, not hers, earned him no thanks from her. He wouldn't want his father to know what a louse he was, would he?

But as those same nerves which she thought she had seen in Catherine, started to get to her, it was just after six when Keely saw that her bright chatter was starting to sound a shade brittle. The last thing she wanted her mother to know was that she was in any way nervous about anything. But, try as she might to concentrate only on the here and now, she found it impossible to keep her thoughts from wandering on to what she had committed herself to and—how on earth did she get out of it?

'Should we be going now?' she asked, turning to see that Tarrant had been indolently watching her.

'Eager to be off?' he enquired laconically, his eyes going meaningfully from her eyes down to her mouth.

'I expect Keely has a date tonight, don't you, Keely?' inserted Lucas, saving her from having to answer Tarrant's question.

'One I can't get out of, unfortunately,' she said brightly, not finding her new stepbrother any more endearing when he remarked:

'The choice was yours, surely?'

Choice! she fumed, sitting beside him in the Ferrari as Lucas and Catherine came to wave them goodbye.

She tried to keep that picture of her mother standing on the steps, safe and secure with Lucas's arm around her, as they waved. She was positive that her mother had looked relieved when she had told her that Tarrant had decided to spend the weekend in London after all.

But, try as she might, the nearer the Ferrari got to London—Tarrant Varley not putting himself out to start any sort of a conversation—the picture of Catherine safe with Lucas was getting harder and harder to conjure back.

By the time Tarrant was pulling up into a salubrious-looking area, her thoughts having gone every which way in trying to find some escape route, Keely had got herself worked up into quite a lather.

Stepping reluctantly out on to the pavement when a mocking Tarrant came round to open the passenger door, a hint she didn't need that he was waiting for her to metaphorically put her money where her mouth was, Keely was seeing only one thing. If she told him exactly what she thought of him, exactly what he could do with any intentions he had once inside that flat, then without any question of a doubt, he would straight away be turning the Ferrari in the direction of the way they had come, and, with the speed he drove, he could be back at Inchbrook in time to join the newly married couple for dinner.

Her nerves were to reach a fine pitch by the time Tarrant had ushered her into his flat. 'Mind if I take a look around?' she asked, wanting to put some distance between them, positive that any moment now he was going to make a grab for her.

'Make yourself at home,' he mocked. Keely didn't need to be told twice.

Her mother had said that Tarrant had a small flat, but as Keely took her time in going from room to room, she saw that while he had only one bedroom—

the one room she chose not to linger in in case Tarrant suddenly appeared from out of nowhere—his flat was spacious, his good quality furniture down to a minimum, giving the whole place a masculine un-cluttered look.

Glancing at her watch as she stood in the dining room, she saw that it was nearing eight. Ample time still for that brute to get back to Inchbrook should she do as everything in her was telling her to do—to get out of there.

A sound from the sitting room had her nerves jumping and saw her leaving her pretended study of an oil painting on one of the walls. Oh God, was he getting impatient! Afraid she would feel his hands on her at any second, those hands dragging her to the bedroom, abruptly Keely left the dining room.

'Nice place you have here,' she opined civilly from the doorway.

'You can let me have a copy of the inventory when you've typed it back,' drawled Tarrant from his relaxed position on the settee.

From that she gathered that he considered that she had been away long enough to have counted every last knife, fork and spoon in his cutlery drawer.

A clap of sudden and unexpected thunder made her jump. She hadn't even noticed that the weather had changed, and that it was now raining.

'Nervous?' mocked her unwanted host.

Knowing his mockery was all on account of him believing she was acting it up for all she was worth, just as he'd accused her of dramatically playing the innocent, it suddenly came to her that she didn't have to take any of it from him. There was no Lucas or Catherine there now for her to have to hide what she was feeling. Why should she be civil to the swine anyway!

'Of you!' she scoffed.

'You misunderstand me,' he replied, unmoved. 'We

both know that you've been this way before, don't we?' And while it was sinking in that in Tarrant Varley's esteemed opinion it was seldom that she spent a weekend alone, be it in her own flat or anyone else's, he was going on to put her right. 'I meant the thunder. Some women of my acquaintance have a decided aversion to thunderstorms.'

Briefly the thought touched down; would she be able to save herself from that fate which used to be reported as a fate worse than death, if she suddenly threw a fit of hysterics because of the thunder and lightning crashing about outside?

But by then Tarrant had risen to his feet and was coming nearer, and every thought went out of her head save that now was the moment when he was going to make a grab for her—and that there was still time for him to make it back to Inchbrook if she voiced any objection!

He was about two yards from her when Keely quickly moved from the doorway. 'Are you hungry?' she asked, and nearly died as she realised he could answer that by saying he was hungry for her body. Rapidly then she was tacking on, 'I'm starving for my dinner. H-have you got anything I can cook for us?'

Her heart pounding so that she thought he must hear it, she saw him halt in his stride.

'Taught at your mother's knee, were you, that the way to a man's heart is through his stomach?' he jibed.

A finger of anger came then to make her feel better; this diabolical man didn't have a heart. 'You could waste away for all I care,' she flared. But her anger speedily departed as she saw that her firing up at him had brought a glint of interest to his eyes. 'I want to eat,' she added flatly.

'The condemned woman ate a hearty meal,' he was back to mocking as he misquoted.

The steak and frozen vegetables Tarrant had found for her in the fridge would, she saw with disappointment, not take any time to cook. And in the instance of welcoming having to cook a banquet, it had still only just gone nine when the food she had no appetite for had been demolished, and she saw that Tarrant's plate also was clear.

Time, she thought, was a perverse creature. When you wanted time to dawdle it went on wings, when you wanted it to fly, it took its rhythm from a tortoise.

With still ample time to kill, she thought that if she could evade Tarrant Varley's clutches till, say, gone ten—no, better make it half past to be on the safe side, for surely he would not return to Inchbrook at that time of night—she could give him a large slice of her mind and then return to her flat entirely unscathed, Keely set about collecting up the used dishes.

'Leave those,' she was ordered abruptly.

'Leave them?' she echoed, her heart starting to drum again as she stood up. She had been planning to make the washing up last her all of half an hour. 'I always clear up after a meal.'

'Not tonight you don't.' Keely avoided letting him see her swallowing, just as she avoided asking why tonight particularly. She already knew the answer to that one; Tarrant Varley thought he had other plans for her. 'Go into the sitting room,' he ordered. 'I'll join you presently.'

Hating him, Keely liked the idea of being by herself for a while, even as she definitely did not like the sound of that 'I'll join you presently'.

Shock hit her in the pit of her stomach when, in less than five minutes, she was sure, Tarrant came to join her. And that shock was nearly bowling her over, because as he came into the room and over to where she was sitting, her mouth went dry to see from his damp hair that he had showered and that his broad shoulders were now covered in nothing more than a brown towelling robe that ended somewhere around his knees.

'What—a splendid idea,' she said, leaving the settee

fast when he came to sit beside her. 'May I—use your bathroom too? I feel a—a little grubby, having been in the same clothes all day.'

His sardonic look told her what he thought of her panicking virgin act. But it was without reference to it that smoothly he replied:

'I thought you might be. That's why I've left a fresh bathrobe for you to change into when you're through.'

Oh God, Keely thought, leaning her hot forehead against the tiled bathroom wall. It was becoming obvious to her then that Tarrant Varley was no catch-and-grab lecher. She had been in his flat for what must be nearly two hours now, and he hadn't so much as laid a finger on her. Why hadn't she seen that before? Oh, if only she had remained seated on that settee she could have found some topic of conversation to engage him in until perhaps another half an hour had gone by. Then, and only then, she could have suggested using his bathroom to freshen herself. He must have thought she would want to do that anyway, or seeing that she didn't have a change of clothes with her, he would not have bothered finding a freshly laundered robe for her.

Having washed her face free of make-up and taken the longest shower of her life, Keely donned the white towelling robe Tarrant had left for her. But on wiping the steam from her watch, she was unable to stifle a groan—it was still only a quarter to ten!

'Are you all right in there? Do you need any help?'

Swine, she thought. 'I'm fine,' she called back quickly, guessing that if he hadn't heard her groan his enquiry was because he considered she had been in his bathroom for long enough.

He was back sitting on the settee when, because for another three-quarters of an hour she had no option but to join him, Keely went in.

'The water's nice and hot,' she said to hide her nerves as she went to pass him to take the armchair at an angle to the left of the settee.

'It usually is,' he murmured, as with an unhurried movement he caught hold of her wrist before she could pass.

Her heart starting up what was now beginning to become a familiar fast beat, Keely found he had exerted just sufficient pressure to have her sitting beside him. Three-quarters of an hour to go, pounded in her head, panic rising when he turned in his seat to look at her.

He still had a hold of her left wrist with his left hand, and her mouth went dry when his right arm moved to rest casually along the back of the settee behind her.

But with her heart racing like charging horses, having guessed all along that she couldn't go through with this, it was then that Keely knew that she was definitely not going to go through with it. But, with the minute hand of her watch ticking around so painfully slowly, the thought came that maybe now, here in his flat, away from Inchbrook and the father he must love as dearly as she loved her mother, so hard had he tried to protect him from grasping women, that he might listen to reason now when he hadn't been prepared to listen to reason before.

It was then that Keely too turned in her seat—turned, and was then ready to once more try her hand at reasoning with him. She had even opened her mouth to begin, but only to close it again, as for the very first time she saw a look in Tarrant's eyes that just had to be admiring. And if that wasn't enough to throw her, she was to find herself startled to hear her name on his lips, a new, more gentle note in his voice, as softly he murmured:

'Do you know, Keely, you're one of the very few women I know who can look as good without make up, as with it.'

'Er...' Some moisture came back to her dried mouth, and with it, some semblance of recovery. 'Not everything about me is as phoney as you believe,' she said, putting all the brightness she was capable of into that statement. If she got him to believe that, it would be a good start in trying to reason with him.

But she had said the wrong thing! She knew it as soon as she saw his mouth quirk, knew it before he said, 'Now there's an invitation for me to find out for myself if ever I heard one.'

And while she stared, and was then in urgent need of leaving that settee, the arm along the back of it had come about her shoulders, the fingers of his right hand gripping her arm and bringing her inexorably closer.

No! she wanted to scream as his head came nearer. But she found she had no time to say anything. For before she could do more than part her lips, she was finding that Tarrant's mouth had claimed hers.

There was still time, said her head when his mouth left hers. 'I thought . . .' she began, but only to be interrupted by his murmured:

'You can tell me your thoughts later,' as he let her know that he just wasn't interested in any of the little gems that had gone through her mind. That it was not her mind which interested him! 'Meantime,' he breathed, 'you look far from comfortable.'

Keely had been in a clinch before, but the expertise of Tarrant Varley was to leave her stunned. Effortlessly he had her feet leaving the ground, and it was to her dismay that she discovered that she was on her back on the settee, the wrap of her robe coming open to reveal that she had opted to stay in her lacy briefs.

'Such modesty!' was his only sarcastic observation, and the next she knew, his length was stretched out on the settee with her!

To feel his lean hard body next to hers, only a couple of layers of towelling separating them, had everything in her screaming that this had gone far enough. But, still shaken to find that she was now lying, where only seconds before she had been sitting, made her delay too long to get any objections she had to make across.

And by then Tarrant, seeing not the slightest sign

about her that she was demurring, promptly proceeded to scatter any tactfully stalling word that had come to her.

The feel of his large hand warmly caressing beneath the material of the loose overlarge robe she had on, as his hand moved to take hold of her naked shoulder, made her want to cry out in protest. But, as before, any sound she had to make was never heard. For his mouth, his lips mobile on hers, were successfully stifling what she had wanted to say. Those lips staying over hers as that hand caressed backwards and forwards over her shoulder.

There's still time to stop him, she thought with part of her mind, while the other part thought, Oh God, it can't be anywhere near half past ten yet!

Fresh panic entered her heart, her stomach region, when Tarrant's kiss deepened. That he had spent none of his thirty-six years anywhere near a monastery was fast being borne in on her. But that panic in her when he drew her body yet closer, his legs mingling with hers, had her jerking on the settee in a spasm of movement, control gone for the moment, instinct only there to motivate her in trying to get away from him.

But, in lifting her body the way she had when that uncontrolled dart of panic had had its way, Keely was to regain some control, only to find that Tarrant had thought she was liking what he was doing to her, and believed that her movement had been only because she wanted even closer body contact.

'You're a hot little thing, aren't you, Keely?' he murmured, taking his lips from hers to seek a sensual area behind her ears. Panic started to riot again, but only to be calmed when, softly, he breathed, 'But there's no need to rush, is there—we have all night.'

When Tarrant kissed her again, Keely had taken succour from his comment. By the sound of it, he was in no desperate hurry to have her body.

It was then that she started to react in the way she

thought she was meant to react. By her reckoning, if he
kept this up for, say, the next half hour, then at the end
of that time, too late she would have thought for him to
return to Inchbrook, she could coolly tell him, 'April
fool'.

She moved her arms from where they had been
making sure her robe did not come open. 'As you say,
Tarrant,' she whispered, keeping her eyes veiled so he
should not see any sign of the triumph she felt, or the
satisfaction that would be hers in half an hour's time to
have fooled him, 'the night is long.' She raised her arms
to put them over his broad-shouldered back. 'Kiss me,'
she smiled, still thinking herself very clever.

Quite when her calculations began to go awry, she
was never really certain. She had been kissed before,
and until Tarrant Varley had begun kissing her, she had
always found that experience moderately enjoyable. But
she had believed that, hating him, it was she who was in
charge of the situation. She who, when the time was
right, was going to have the beautiful satisfaction of
saying 'By-ee', his kisses having no effect on her
whatsoever, suddenly, Keely was starting to feel the
oddest of sensations.

It must have begun, she was to try and pinpoint later,
from the moment Tarrant had felt what he assumed
were her willing arms around him. For gradually, the
tenor of his kisses began to change. Slowly at first, his
mouth gentle on hers, he began piece by piece to draw a
response from her.

At that stage Keely was sure she was only responding
because, if this love play was to go on for the half hour
it had to, if she did not show some response, of a
certainty he was going to know about it.

But, panic trying to get a hold a third time as his
hand caressed away from her shoulder and towards her
breasts, Keely could not help but grip him hard.

Grey eyes were then staring into green eyes, as that
hand on her silky skin stilled. And she saw then that if

she didn't relax a little, she was going to blow the whole thing.

'Got a crick in my neck,' she invented as she felt panic of a different sort. Relax, idiot! she told herself. Any more moves like that, as if she was protesting, would soon have Tarrant Varley rumbling her. 'You have lovely warm hands,' she purred, and stretched up to kiss him.

When Tarrant needed no further prompting, Keely put all she had into that kiss. But his reaction to the way she pushed her fingers through his hair as she held him to her startled her into an awareness that he was finding yet more passion from a seemingly limitless supply—that passion creating in her that odd sensation she had felt before, but which this time was a sensation that was stretching out and growing!

It was a slightly confused Keely who looked back at Tarrant the next time he raised his head. 'Be patient,' he instructed softly, as he read the look in her eyes.

Her confusion was in no way diminished when he kissed her again and she felt his hands move to caress the full globes of her breasts. For suddenly she was realising that when she had had to make an effort to relax before, had had to give herself stern instructions to relax, she had now taken so well to the part she was playing that she had relaxed without having to think about it at all.

Tarrant's mouth left hers to trace kisses down her throat and across her chest, but it was when she felt his mouth at her naked breasts that Keely became alive to danger. For when a small moan left her at the mind-blowing things his lips were doing to the raised pink tip of her breast, she was to know belatedly that her moan had been involuntary, that he was succeeding in stirring her blood like no man before had ever succeeded in doing!

'Tarrant!' she choked. But when his hand took the place of his mouth, took over the caressing of her

breast, she was too confused to remember what she had
wanted to say.

It was then, as if he knew how it was with her, that he
did not wait for her to get her thoughts together. It was
then that he kissed her again. And it was then when he
kissed her, drawing a matching passion from her, that
Keely forgot everything but that—she wanted him.

'Love me,' she breathed, without knowing that she
had spoken.

But as Tarrant renewed his onslaught to her mouth,
to kiss and caress not just her breasts, but her back, her
spine, her hips, her thighs, saluting with kisses where his
hands caressed, many minutes were to tick by before it
looked as though she was going to get her desire.

And by that time he had driven her to such a fever
pitch of wanting that she was barely aware of
movement as, effortlessly, his mouth lingering over
hers, he picked her up and started to carry her from the
room.

With her arms around his neck as he carried her,
when he paused to open the bedroom door, she wanted
his mouth back on hers. And in a no-man's-land, a land
she had never thought to be so blood-stirring, so
beautiful, a land where she wanted to stay, yet wanted
more, much much more, Keely's thinking was nowhere
about when she heard him murmur some nebulous
question about had she taken the necessary preventive
measures?

They were inside the bedroom, when, her mouth
starved for his kisses, she opened her eyes to see that by
his look, Tarrant was not going to kiss her again until
she had answered his question.

Nowhere near sure what his question had been, so
fired by him was she by his kisses, all she wanted was
that question out of the way so she could again feel his
all-consuming touch.

'Preventive—measures?' she whispered, all the answer
he could want there as she tried with what thinking

power she had left to discover what he was asking, the sooner to get back to where he had taken her. 'I don't . . .' know what you mean, she would have ended, had she had the chance.

Only she did not get the chance. For suddenly Tarrant had immediately read all that he wanted to know in her answer. And as suddenly, just as though she was an armful of hot coals he was carrying, he had thrown her from him.

Hitting the mattress with a bump, her shining dark hair bouncing with her, Keely blinked as the centre light was switched on. But she was nowhere near to getting her senses when:

'My God!' she heard Tarrant snarl, all the confirmation she could need in his face that something had gone very wrong, as his voice snarling still, he flung at her, 'You're a cool one!'

All Keely was capable of was to sit where she had landed, her eyes staring as, her voice husky, she stammered, completely bewildered, 'I don't—understand.'

'Not much you don't,' he rapped grimly, his eyes icy where before she would have sworn that they had held warmth for her. 'Seeing your mother hook a man who can give her a life of luxury, you saw no reason why you shouldn't try for the same. Tough luck, sweetheart,' he tossed at her. 'I'm not so easily ensnared!'

Stunned by this turn of events, all she could do was to stare dumbly as she tried to gather her scattered wits together. His mention of her mother was of no help in that, her face growing pink, Keely realised that she hadn't given thought to her mother in the Lord knew how long! But while it was starting to become clearer by the second that Tarrant Varley was accusing her of trying to get her hooks into him the same way that her mother had got her hooks into his father, her thinking power had so far been sent flying that all she could wonder from that remark was that if with her cooking

Catherine had ensnared Lucas, then by what method was Tarrant suggesting that she herself was out to entrap him?

'I've been wondering all evening what your angle was,' he went on when, still trying to dissect his remark, Keely hadn't said anything. 'Now,' he said succinctly, 'I know.'

'You—know,' she said slowly, wishing he would hurry up and tell her. Never had she felt so utterly bereft of intelligence.

'You're a passionate little thing when your blood is fired, aren't you?' he said, not requiring an answer, as sarcastically he continued. 'But you really will have to learn to have your answers off pat—to temper that passion with the cool head with which you do your plotting, Miss Macfarlane.'

Starting at last to surface on hearing that after all that had happened between them, she was now back to being Miss Macfarlane; but worse than that; that while she had been lost to anything but his lovemaking Tarrant, by the sound of it, had kept a cool head the whole time, Keely was to be rocked to her very foundations to hear his voice loaded with sarcasm, as he went on:

'My apologies for your wasted efforts—such a shame that your plan to trap me into fatherhood didn't come off.'

'Fatherhood!'

Shock had her making a spasm of movement that jerked open her robe. But as she saw his cold eyes go to the creamy swell of her uncovered breast before she could hastily pull the folds of her robe together, Keely was to experience an even greater shock. Streaking in then came the meaning behind his question of, had she taken the necessary preventive measures! Oh, my God, she thought, feeling ready to faint as only then did she become aware that had it not been for the fact that Tarrant Varley had been able to keep his loathsome cool head, then she might well have ended up pregnant!

With shock waves lashing her that, now that her body heat had returned to being somewhere near to normal, she should have forgotten what had been in her mind at the start of their lovemaking, Keely's throat felt too paralysed for her to speak. To know that he had, without any great effort, had her so mindless that all thoughts on her mother's happiness had been driven from her mind, left her momentarily speechless. Though the thought that the hateful Tarrant Varley could have had her so completely under his spell that, to her mortification, he had been able to find the key to unsuspected chemistry in her, and that she should have been willing to be so intimate with him that she could have conceived his child, released her locked throat and had her babbling angrily in her urgency to answer his charge.

'You must be insane!' she exclaimed in a rush, stunned into silence for so long, words now queuing up to be hurled at him. 'Why, apart from the fact that the women in my family have too long a history of being sick from the word go when they start on the trail of parenthood, I should need more than the few hours' notice I've had before I would even voluntarily think of disabling myself for months on end. And you,' she said hotly, 'would be the last man I'd consider to . . .'

'You'd got your mind made up inside two minutes,' she was cut off shortly. 'You were more than ready to incapacitate yourself if by so doing it meant you could ensnare me into marriage.'

'Marriage!' Keely pushed fresh shock aside. 'Lord help us,' she gasped, 'they don't make medals big enough for the one I should need to take you on!' And, in disbelief as it suddenly dawned on her what he was saying! 'You're that honourable!' she exclaimed scornfully.

But her scorn did not so much as dent him, and

suddenly Keely felt she'd had enough. Some time later she knew she was going to be unable to avoid a private post-mortem on the incredulous way she had been with the swine. But right this minute, she reckoned she had done more than any daughter could be expected to do to ensure that her parent's marriage got off without an unwanted third party present.

What the time was then, as she hot-footed it from the bed, was neither here nor there. Clutching the folds of the robe about her, its hem flapping against her legs, with all the dignity she could muster she announced:

'I'm going.'

Her head in the air, she had made it to the open doorway and into the hall before Tarrant's voice halted her:

'It's tipping down outside.'

Keely turned, hate for him in her eyes to see him leaning casually against the post of the door. 'So?' she snapped.

'You'll never get a taxi—especially this time of a Saturday night.'

From swine, he turned quickly to being a reptile that after making so free with her—she was angry enough then to overlook her willingness to be made free with at the time—he had no intention of driving her home.

'I'll walk,' she said tightly, and would have turned then to go to the bathroom where she had left her clothes.

'Suit yourself,' he replied toughly. 'But . . .' she hesitated, '. . . but you'll get drenched and very likely ruin that pink thing you came in.'

'So!' Keely snapped. 'Have you a better suggestion— since you obviously aren't going to give me the loan of a raincoat?'

Tarrant shrugged, his manner that of take it or leave it, it was all the same to him, as he offered, 'You can have the bed if you like.'

'I'm underwhelmed,' she scoffed. 'And just where are you going to sleep?'

She did not care at all for the insolent way his eyes went over her the moment before he drawled, 'Even with all your—charms—well remembered, Miss Macfarlane, I still prefer my freedom.'

Oh, wouldn't she just love to pull him down a peg or two! But in the absence of that, remembering his long length on his settee, Keely felt she might be going some way to seeing him fall flat on his face, if she accepted his offer. That settee was all very well for a short burst of lovemaking, but he'd soon wish he'd kept his mouth shut if he had to spend a night on it!

'A gentleman to the last,' she threw in his direction, and moved towards him, owning disappointment that he didn't look surprised that she should be taking him up on his offer. Though when he stepped out of the way and fully out into the hall to allow her entrance into the bedroom, Keely did feel some small degree of satisfaction in that she was able to about turn and slam the door shut in his face.

There was nothing more she wanted to say to that unbearable monster, she considered as, tucking the folds of her robe round her, she climbed into the big bed. In fact, if she had her way, never would she so much as speak to him again.

The night was long in passing, and her sleep fitful. Though undisturbed by any unwanted visitor, Keely was again awake as dawn broke.

She pondered then on the absence of a visit from her host. Not that he would have succeeded in getting her anywhere near the way he had got her before. God, when she thought of how she had been! Quickly Keely hopped back to thinking of Tarrant and how he could have been glued to that settee through the night for all she had seen or heard of him.

But she was surprised when it was borne in on her that, whatever else she might think of him, one fact

stood out from all others—Tarrant Varley *was* an
honourable man!

Had he not been honourable, she saw, he would not
have cared a button for that risk of giving her a child.
He had wanted her, she knew that, even if he had kept a
cool head when she had been mindless to anything but
her need. But aside from that physical wanting, he
hated her as much as she hated him. And with that
honour ingrained in him—probably inherited from his
father—no matter how strong was Tarrant Varley's
desire, there was no way he was going to risk having to
pay by, according to his code, having to marry her, was
there?

Leaving the bed, Keely went to look out of the
window. At some time during the night it had stopped
raining, she saw. Well, thank you for the bed, and
goodbye, Mr Varley, she thought, as she tiptoed her
way to the bathroom.

Though once dressed and ready to be on her way,
Keely experienced the most strange reluctance to depart
without seeing Tarrant once more. Must be a devil for
punishment, she decided, putting that urge down to
some self-punitive streak in her that she should want to
see again the face of that monster in the sitting room.

But that urge was not to be denied as stealthily she
crept in to look at the figure on the couch which was
covered by a solitary blanket.

He was quite good-looking, she observed, that stern
expression he usually reserved for her absent in sleep.
Her glance went from his high intelligent forehead, to
his determined though stubbly chin, to see, with a
feeling akin to surprise, that in sleep his mouth took on
a warm, generous shape.

Quite unaccountably, her heart skipped a beat as her
thoughts roved to wonder if that mouth would ever
have that kind look when he was awake and talking to
her.

Scorning that the day would ever come, Keely turned

and went from the sitting room. Apart from the fact that she was never going to see him again if she could help it, why for goodness' sake should it matter a row of beans to her whether his mouth was kind or not when he spoke to her?

CHAPTER FOUR

HER mother had been married to Lucas for four weeks before Keely was at last able to come to terms with, and cease to constantly wonder at, the never before experienced avalanche of wanting that Tarrant Varley had so astonishingly been able to draw from her.

That it had taken so long to rid herself of thoughts of her amazing reaction to his lovemaking was, she was able to realise then, only because she had afterwards been utterly appalled to remember the way she had been. To think that she too, like anyone else—everyone except Tarrant Varley, that was—could go so far as to lose her cool when plain common or garden sex reared its ugly head, had been an unprepared-for eye-opener to her. But what made it worse, and had her examining the Keely Macfarlane she had always thought she was, was the fact that she did not even *like* the man!

But at the end of those four weeks, she was some way to salving her humiliation at the way she would have freely given herself to a man she loathed. By then she was able to console herself that, on pins as she had been all the time lest the smallest word or action out of place ruined her mother's day, she had been too emotionally on edge to put up much of a fight when Tarrant Varley had hotted up his expert lovemaking.

But in having put the whole episode down to experience of life, and vowing that never again would she get herself into that position, Keely, though she had spoken many times on the phone to her mother, still retained sufficient scar tissue not to want Tarrant Varley to feature in any of those telephone conversations.

Which had to make her think that she was the most

contradictory of creatures. For on a Friday a week later, Catherine having been married to Lucas for five weeks, Keely was about to replace the phone on another of those telephone conversations with her mother, when from nowhere the question popped out:

'Have you seen anything of Tarrant recently?'

'He didn't come home last weekend,' replied Catherine, sounding cheerful. 'Though he phones his father regularly.'

When she finally said goodbye, Keely sighed that, unwittingly, she had prompted another request that she should visit Inchbrook for a weekend soon; a request she had wanted to avoid.

Wondering for how much longer she could put off accepting that invitation to Inchbrook, Keely went on to think that if Tarrant was going to take to spending the odd weekend at his flat, then maybe she could fit in a weekend when she was sure he would not be there? Obviously she wanted to see her mother, but she had no wish whatsoever to renew her acquaintance with that brute!

The week following was to see her again giving too much of her thinking time up to Tarrant Varley. So that by the time the next weekend hoved into sight, she was beginning to wish she had never enquired about him or discovered that he had spent one weekend at least in that never-to-be-forgotten flat.

That he did not feel compelled to spend every weekend at Inchbrook made her wonder then—was it because he was having second thoughts about her mother having designs on his father's fortune? Was he having second thoughts about needing to be there to pick up the pieces when the scales dropped from his father's eyes? Or was it that he had other fish to fry?

That last thought made Keely frown. Not that it worried her in the least whom he took back to his flat, whom he took to his bed, she was sure of that. But again she was dratting the man that, having had him out of her mind for a few days, a few days was all it had been.

Not being as busy as usual at the office that Friday, Keely pulled the finished typing matter from her machine, and on impulse, picked up the phone and dialled Inchbrook. Since she and her mother had fallen into a pattern of ringing each other alternately, and it was her turn now since Catherine had rung her a week ago, Keely was ready for a chat.

'Are you all right?' was Catherine's first motherly question, for seldom was it that her daughter rang her from the office.

'I'm fine,' Keely laughed, explaining that things were slack at the moment. 'How are things with you?'

'Couldn't be better,' was the reply, to give Keely a warm glow inside that her mother was sounding on top of the world.

'Married life seems to suit you,' she commented.

'Lucas is a darling,' said Catherine happily.

'And Tarrant?' Appalled that the question, without any known volition from her, seemed to have just slipped out, Keely could have groaned aloud.

'He was at Inchbrook last Saturday,' said Catherine, her voice sounding happy still, when Keely had been on the way to thinking that she had just put her foot in it by reminding her of her brute of a stepson.

'He was there for the weekend?' her wayward tongue went on to ask.

'Unfortunately not,' replied Catherine. 'He only came for a few hours on Saturday to . . .'

'Unfortunately!' The exclamation could not be held in. 'Do you mean you actually—*like* having him there?'

'I have no wish to drive Tarrant out of his home, Keely,' said Catherine a shade sharply, but relented quickly. 'Oh, you're thinking of that money he tried to give me to leave, aren't you,' going on to confess, just like old times, with no secrets between them, 'I have to own that Tarrant's insult in trying to give me that cheque did make me a little apprehensive about how things were going to work out. But everything's fine now that I fully understand that it was only out of love for his father that Tarrant did what he tried to do.'

That her mother was ready to forgive that insult; and even seemed to have been on the way to forgetting it, was more than Keely would ever do. Nothing in her book excused for an instant that he had callously, deliberately insulted someone she loved dearly.

But, as if she *had* forgotten that Tarrant had ever tried to get her out, Catherine was going on with some domestic tale of how the way the marmalade she had made in January was going, it didn't look likely to last until the Seville oranges were again in the shops next January. And Keely was hearing sounds in the next office that told her Gerald was on the move. That sound reminded her that she was at work and that her chat with her mother looked like being one of the extended type such as they sometimes had when she was using her own phone.

'I shall have to go, darling,' she said, when Catherine had finished with the marmalade and before she could go on to another subject. 'We'll chat again . . .'

'When are you coming to Inchbrook?' came the question she had been hoping to avert. 'I shall begin to think you've taken against Lucas if you don't come and visit us soon.'

'I think he's a love, and you know I do,' said Keely quickly. That his son headed her 'Beast of the year' poll was another matter.

'Then come and visit us this weekend,' said Catherine promptly. 'Tarrant has to work this weekend because he's going abroad on a business trip on Monday—we'd like at least *one* of our children with us.'

Gerald had come to stand in the doorway, but what Catherine had said about Tarrant not going to Inchbrook tomorrow, was all Keely needed to know.

'Would I deprive you of seeing your one and only,' she said cheekily.

'You'll come?'

Suddenly Keely was as eager to see her mother as she sounded eager to see her. 'Expect me some time tomorrow,' she bubbled.

Gerald strolled over to her desk the minute she put down the phone. 'You've got something on for tomorrow?' he questioned, his slightly hangdog expression giving her a clue that he might have been going to ask her out himself.

'I'm going to spend the weekend with my mother and her husband,' replied Keely, having informed him before the wedding about her mother marrying Lucas.

'I was rather hoping you would come out with me tomorrow night,' he didn't give up. 'I've only just managed to get some tickets for . . .'

'Sorry, Gerald,' said Keely, still no clearer on what she was going to do about him. 'I haven't seen my mother since the wedding, and I've hardly had a chance to get to know Lucas.'

'You've hardly given yourself chance to get to know me either,' he grumbled.

'I see you every day,' she told him quietly, starting to feel uncomfortable. She didn't want to hurt his feelings, but if he couldn't see that what she knew of him was all she wanted to know of him, then short of being blunt and probably having to resign from a job she liked, she saw that he was never going to.

'Monday to Friday,' he complained, 'with the occasional concession to my taking you out.' Since she felt that the moment was coming ever nearer when she was just going to have to be blunt and hurt his feelings, suddenly, and to her relief, Gerald was smiling. 'I tell you what—why don't I drive you to the Varley place? The Maserati could do with a run.'

Keely went home from the office that night to cook herself a meal, do a few chores and pack what she would need for the weekend. It had been weak of her to accept Gerald's offer of a lift when she could just as easily have gone by train, she thought as she folded into her case a knee-length dinner gown which would suffice whether Lucas was into dressing for dinner or if he wasn't. But what else could she have done, with Gerald's face showing his disappointment that she wasn't going to go the theatre with him?

Fifteen minutes before the appointed time, the front door to the flats where Keely lived being open as it usually was in summer, Gerald had mounted the stairs to her first floor flat, and was knocking on her door.

Fortunately she was ready, and although she invited him in, it was for no longer than it took for her to collect her suitcase from her bedroom, then they were off.

But at Inchbrook, when Gerald stated that he had nothing planned for the afternoon, Catherine, being Catherine, wouldn't hear of anything but that he stayed for lunch. Which left Keely fending off, as best she could, his affectionte glances across the table; glances which she was sure were not being missed by either her mother or Lucas.

Gerald was in no hurry to leave once the meal was over either, but adjourned with them to the drawing room. By this time, though, Lucas, before Tarrant had taken over, having chaired an industry related to the work Gerald's firm did, had let fall about his workshop at the back of the house, complete with a lathe and other machinery, where he still dabbled in engineering.

Seeing that the two men were soon engrossed in things mechanical, Keely's eyes went to her mother, and joy welled up in her to see that Catherine did indeed look as happy as she had sounded on the telephone. Her eyes then went to Lucas, who had that same look of inner contentment on his face, just as he was saying:

'Will you excuse us, my dear—Keely? Gerald here would like to see my workshop.'

'And you can't wait to show it off,' teased Catherine—and Keely just loved that sheepish, love-filled grin he gave her mother.

'They're going to be ages, you know that, don't you?' said Catherine once they had gone. 'Thank goodness Lucas has a wash basin in his workshop, or I'd have a permanent black grease mark around my kitchen sink!'

Keely laughed, never remembering her mother being so houseproud before. 'You love it here, don't you?' she stated.

Catherine nodded, though she qualified, 'Not that it would mean very much without that dear man. But all this, the house, the gardens, and Lucas too—who could want for anything more?' And not waiting for her daughter's reply, for in truth, with her mother's happiness shining from her, a reply wasn't needed, suddenly Catherine was remembering, 'You haven't had chance to see the gardens yet, have you?' And, motherly all at once, 'You go out and get some fresh air. Take a look around while I tidy up a bit in the kitchen.'

About to give an obedient if a touch impish, 'Yes, Mother,' Keely changed her mind. 'Can't I give you a hand?' she asked.

'There isn't a lot for me to do. You go out into the garden and get some colour into your cheeks,' Catherine ordered.

'Colour!' exclaimed Keely, pretending to look scandalised. 'I'll have you know that men go overboard when they see complexions like mine!'

'So why haven't you presented me with a son-in-law yet?' replied Catherine with a grin at her sauce.

'Good question,' answered Keely, and by way of the French doors, went out into the gardens as she had been instructed.

But out in the gardens, with immaculate lawns spread out before her, flowers of every hue opening their petals wide to the late May sunshine, it was to the left of the lawns that Keely turned. A clump of shrubbery backed by tall nut trees attracted her attention as she thought about her mother's joking remark about why hadn't she presented her with a son-in-law.

Was her mother anxious to see her married? It was the first intimation she had given, if that were so, she mused as she stepped from the path and into the shrubbery.

The splash of colour from her red dress contrasted brightly like holly berries as she moved among the green leaves to the trees, her thoughts going to the opportunities to take a husband which she had turned her back on.

One or two men she had been friends with had possessed that extra something which might have seen her growing fond of them had she given herself the chance. But did she want marriage? Did she want marriage and everything that went with marriage? And, remembering the Butterworth Factor—did she want children?

Was it unnatural of her to view motherhood—or rather the nine months leading up to that state—as something she would have to want desperately before she went in for it? If she took after the Butterworth line and not the pea-shelling Macfarlane line, she would have to be body and soul in love with some man to want to go through all that to give him a child. And to date, no man she knew had been worth taking the risk of finding out if she had inherited the Butterworth Factor.

Keely was to catch herself up short as a picture of Tarrant Varley took it upon itself to flash into her mind. God, to think . . . She blinked, horrified, and the picture vanished—but not the memory that she had been so mindless with him that she could have put herself in that self-same situation she partly feared, had he not called a halt—and with a man she hated!

A sound heard behind her, a man's tread, made her gratefully leave her thoughts. Indeed, so grateful was she that, guessing Gerald had come to find her, whether he misread the welcome from her thoughts in her smile or not, she could not refrain from beaming a smile as she turned.

'Gerald,' she said, smiling hugely. 'That didn't take as long as . . .'

Abruptly she broke off, her mind playing the strangest of tricks to prove that it had not quite ousted the picture of Tarrant Varley from its sight. For it was Tarrant Varley's mocking face that stared back at her, and she knew perfectly well that he was in London this weekend preparing for his trip abroad on Monday.

Again she blinked. But there was no blinking away when she opened her eyes, that that mocking face was still before her.

'*You!*' she gasped, shock knocking her sideways to see that Tarrant Varley was no figment of her imagination.

'Sorry to disappoint,' was the sardonic reply from the man who should, according to her mother, be hard at work in London.

But while she was still coming to terms with the fact that, try and avoid him as she had, he must have caught sight of her and, in his arrogance, he had seen no reason to consider avoiding her, he was going on to drawl:

'I see from the Maserati that you've brought your crock of gold with you.' And if that wasn't sufficient of an insult, while Keely was still gasping not only from the suddenness of seeing him when that was the last thing she had wanted, he was adding the lofty enquiry, 'Pregnant yet?'

Aghast at his insolence, she got as far as, 'What . . .' before he cut in sarcastically:

'Surely by now you've let Cullen *persuade* you into his bed?'

It was at that point that her pride and anger came storming to the rescue. And any lengthy wonderings she might have had on why was Tarrant Varley at

Inchbrook when he ought to be in London were shelved as she caught his implication that the only way she was going to get any man to marry her was by her first getting that man to give her a child.

She moved then, brushing rudely past Tarrant as she sneered with tight control—that or shove him into the nearest bush, 'Gerald Cullen does have several advantages over you, I must admit—not least that to go with his crock of gold, he has a pleasing personality!'

Keely then found that she did not have time to feel even the smallest glimmer of satisfaction from letting him know that in the personality stakes, Tarrant Varley had the charm of a skunk. For before she could get round him, she felt his firm masculine hand take charge of her arm, and suddenly she was spun round so that she was facing the direction in which she was not intending to go.

'I don't doubt that your estimable employer knows how to flatter a girl,' he tossed at her, his eyes flicking over her shoulder and back again to the mutiny sparking in hers that said it was still on the cards that he might soon be taking a header into the shrubbery. 'But tell me, can he stir you—like this?'

Before she knew what was happening, or even how it had happened, suddenly she was in his arms. And before she could so much as blink, no time there for her to hiss a few uncomplimentary names, his mouth had fastened over hers, and anything she would have said never had the chance to be voiced.

Not that she took to his kissing her without a fight. Not at first, that was. For push and shove at him as she did initially, all without making the smallest headway in gaining her release, suddenly it was all changing. The feel of Tarrant's fingers going down over her spine, the sensuous feel of his body against hers through the thin material of her summer dress, caused all sorts of wayward feelings she did not want to make themselves felt.

No, said her mind, this is crazy, I don't even like the man. But some treachery was at work within her to feel him this close, to have his fingers tracing her spine; so that whatever instructions her head was trying to pass on, somehow those instructions were being diverted and not getting through at all.

So it was that when Tarrant's hold on her slackened a little and his kiss softened to ask for her response rather than demand it, Keely found herself melting. The hands that had been trying to push him away were all at once holding, not pushing, as she gave him her lips.

When Tarrant broke his kiss, her mind was blank of all thought as she stared up at him. But that was only until she saw those grey eyes flick past her over her shoulder and she witnessed that the next time he looked at her there was an unmistakable look of triumph in his eyes. Triumph he did not attempt to hide. Triumph which at first she thought stemmed from nothing more than the easy way he had got her from being a struggling woman in his arms to a pliant one.

But if that wasn't enough to make her pride soar as her blood temperature cooled when, without comment, he turned her to face the way she had been going to go, so as he turned her to face the house and the stone footpath, her blood temperature was to accelerate and go shooting up a very different avenue.

'*You swine!*' she hissed, in sudden fury to see that not too many yards away Gerald was standing and staring incredulously at them. 'You knew damn well he was there!' she raged, knowing from the dejected way Gerald turned and walked towards where he had parked his car that he had witnessed her response to Tarrant.

'I cannot deny it,' Tarrant owned, like some newborn George Washington, though with not a sign of guilt about him. In fact, there was nothing about him to say he was feeling anything but immense enjoyment from the situation he had created.

Her anger too much for her, Keely gave him a shove that should have sent him flying, only which, to her chagrin, did not. And not wasting her breath on more words, she left him, to go charging after Gerald.

But her fury with Tarrant was forced to take a back seat when she rounded the side of the house. For Gerald was in his car and already on the move. She knew that she had hurt her employer, and that hurt her, for never willingly, with the exception of one person, would she have hurt anyone.

Gerald halted the car when he saw her racing up to it, but his face was showing his hurt, without his usual faultless manners gone into hiding in that he refused to get out of the car as she approached the open window.

'I'm—sorry,' was all Keely could think of to say, suddenly feeling totally inadequate.

Her apology was sulkily brushed aside. 'Is he staying the weekend too?' was all he wanted to know.

'No,' she answered, hoping that would make him feel better, and hoping to make him feel better still. 'He's going abroad on Monday and has to go back to London to clear up some loose ends. He's only popped down to see his father for an hour or two,' she added— but wished she hadn't, as Gerald gave her a sceptical look at the suggestion that it was his father whom Tarrant was there to see. Though he did manage the politeness, before he drove off, of:

'I'll see you on Monday.'

Feeling not only saddened, but sick inside too, slowly Keely wandered indoors. It made her unhappy that she had upset Gerald the way she had. It couldn't have been very nice for him that when she had been at pains to keep him at arm's length on the occasions she had gone out with him, he should see her in Tarrant's arms and obviously enjoying being there too. But what sickened her more than anything was that Tarrant Varley, thinking she was on more familiar terms with Gerald than she was, had only kissed her in order that

Gerald should see that she was anybody's, just as though she was some—some tramp!

Finding her mother in the kitchen and alone, although it was important to Keely that Catherine did not see that anything was amiss, she just could not hold back from putting an inflection of a question in her voice as she said:

'I've just seen Tarrant—I thought he was working over the weekend?'

'So he was,' replied Catherine with a smile. 'But when he rang last night and heard from Lucas that you were coming today, he must have thought he could do the work he was going to do on the long flight to Australia.'

'You mean he's—that Tarrant intends to stay the weekend?' Keely questioned, trying to keep a shrill note out of her voice.

But Catherine was not seeing that her daughter was only just this side of horrified at the idea, but was looking more contented than ever as she answered:

'Yes. Now isn't that nice of him? He really is trying to make up for the way he reacted initially to Lucas and me getting married isn't he? He's proving it by abandoning work that's important to him purely so that he can get to know his new stepsister.'

On that instant, Keely made up her mind that if Tarrant Varley was staying the weekend, then she was off. But just as she was sorting out the best way to acquaint her mother with the news that she had changed her mind and would be back to London on the next train, Catherine interrupted her thinking:

'I told Gerald you were in the garden when he popped his head in to say goodbye—has he gone?'

'He left a few minutes ago,' Keely confirmed.

'Did he see Tarrant before he left?'

'Yes, he saw him,' she replied. But she was to know her first experience of ice cold anger when her mother smiled, and said:

'Good. I told Tarrant when he arrived that Gerald had given you a lift and was looking for you—he said he'd come and say "Hello".'

He'd come to say 'Hello' all right, Keely quietly frosted over. Clearly she saw then how it had been. Tarrant Varley, in that cold dispassionate way she was familiar with, had *deliberately* set her up. Knowing that Gerald was looking for her, he had taken a short cut, and had lost no time in hauling her into his arms. He had *known* that Gerald was bound to come up on them—why, she thought as the ice of cold anger cut deeper, he had most likely been kissing her with his eyes open, the better to watch for Gerald! No wonder he hadn't denied knowing that Gerald had been there—he would have been disappointed if he hadn't been—if he'd had to kiss her for nothing!

'All right if I go up to my room for a while?' she asked Catherine, unaware of when she had changed her mind about leaving, aware only of that something in her that chillingly, stonily, made her determined that this time Tarrant was not going to get away with it.

'This is your home too now,' said Catherine softly, and coaxed, 'Try and get used to the idea.'

Keely smiled, but could not think of Inchbrook as her home, nor would she ever while Inchbrook still had a son of the house.

'Don't forget—we dine at eight,' reminded Catherine as Keely left the kitchen.

'I won't,' she promised.

She had been glad to make her escape. Her mother knew her better than anyone. Though since this was the first time Keely had ever experienced ice-cold anger, she was doubtful that Catherine would have recognised that emotion in her for what it was had she stayed longer.

That cold fury was to stay with Keely as she unpacked the few things she had brought with her. And it was to intensify as she went into the adjoining bathroom and experienced the luxury of wallowing in a deep and wide bath with no need to hurry.

How dared Tarrant Varley set her up in the disgusting way he had? How dared he? Just as if she were of no account, she seethed grimly. How dared he let her mother and Lucas believe that the only reason he had abandoned his work this weekend was that he wanted to get to know her better—so he could be a sort of big brother to her? She knew damn well why he had thought a visit home this weekend was far more important than any work he had to do.

It did nothing for the hot ice of fury that reached every part of her, to know that Tarrant Varley's only reason for coming to Inchbrook when he had been acquainted with the news that she would be there was so that he could watch her and keep tabs on her. That he gave no credence to the love she had for her mother and saw her visit to Inchbrook, with him safely out of the way, as purely a visit where she could get her hands on whatever was going, made her hate him with an energy that was almost frightening to her, but not quite.

In Keely's view, it was more than about time she settled a few old scores with one Tarrant Varley. To her mind he, with his cold dispassion, had had things his own way for far too long. Pride, if nothing else, demanded that she had her retribution.

Stepping out of her bath, wrapped in the fluffiest of large towels, Keely knew one thing at least, that she welcomed feeling as she did now. While she felt like this, coldly angry, impenetrable, never would Tarrant Varley get under her guard. Should he take it into his head now to kiss her, then no way would that—God knew what it was, but that certain something of his that made her legs weak, her weak—have a chance.

Not that he would kiss her again. He hadn't wanted to kiss her in the garden, that was now all too obvious. No matter what passion he had put into his kisses, those kisses had been given with an inner dispassion, his mind only on the task he had set himself, no matter how distasteful to him it had been to kiss her, that task of setting her up.

By the time she was dressed she had deliberated long and hard about all that had happened. Had discovered she had too much spirit to be prepared to passively take all that Tarrant Varley thought he could say and do.

Who the hell gave him the right to think he could trample all over her and get off scot free? By God, she was going to get even with him if it took her a year! she vowed.

Her mother's happiness with Lucas was now secure, she had seen that for herself. Nothing Tarrant could do, or herself either, could touch Catherine and Lucas and the contentment they had found with each other, she could be sure of that.

Though how she was going to start getting back at Tarrant Varley was not yet clear to her. But as, still coldly angry, Keely paced her room, she was certain of one thing—if she saw so much as half a chance to set Tarrant Varley up the way he had set her up, then wasn't she going to grasp it—with both hands too!

CHAPTER FIVE

KEELY delayed going down the stairs until her watch showed one minute to eight. Then, knowing she was looking good in her burnt orange dress that contrasted favourably with her colouring, she left her room.

With the hope that whoever was in charge of such matters they would not make her wait a year before they presented her with an opportunity to get her own back on Tarrant Varley, she opened the door of the drawing room.

'You've cut it a bit fine for a pre-dinner drink,' murmured Catherine mildly as Keely, noting that the man who had left his work to come to spy on her was there, smiled her 'Good evenings'.

'Not at all, my dear,' said Lucas. 'What will you have, Keely?'

'Nothing, thank you,' she answered, studiously avoiding looking at Tarrant again, because just seeing him had the effect of heating the ice of her anger with him. And she didn't want that, knowing for a fact that only by being coldly angry could she deal with the mocking devil.

'Then shall we have dinner?' smiled Lucas, doing her heart good to see the fond look he gave her mother.

Keeping her distance from Tarrant, who so far had not addressed one word to her, Keely followed in the wake of Catherine and Lucas to take her place at the table.

That Lucas was a good conversationalist, and often able to make her mother laugh, made the meal progress without either of the recently married pair being aware that the son of the house was saying very little.

Though Keely was aware of it. And all her hate vibes

were going out in his direction that, by the look of it, he couldn't even be bothered to put himself out to speak to her mother. When an inner fairness tried to nudge that since she herself had said little to his father, Tarrant could well be thinking the same about her, Keely refused to heed it. Tarrant Varley knew damn well that she had accepted his father as her mother's husband, she smouldered, her blood temperature starting to rise. She was then to see the precise reason why he was at Inchbrook this weekend. The only reason he had come home was to check that she didn't wheedle her way into getting from his father the same pickings which a true daughter of Lucas might be entitled to expect.

It became almost unendurable then that it looked as if she was going to have a long wait to get even with him. And as talk at the table became sporadic, so she willed the coldness she needed back to her anger.

As she did her best to do justice to the meal, it was as the main course neared an end that Lucas appeared to notice that she had had very little to say. And having obviously searched for something which would bring her into the conversation, causing her again to think what a super person he was, she was to leave her thoughts on what she would like to do to his un-super son, when Lucas smilingly remarked:

'Your employer seems a sound chap, Keely.'

'He is,' she smiled back, trying hard, since Lucas had made an effort to get her talking, to think of something else to say about Gerald.

But Lucas, perhaps thinking that she was shy on the subject of her boss, was there to help her out again as he teased, having not missed the way Gerald had looked at her a time or two:

'It passed my mind that he might be staying to dinner.'

The table the four of them were sat round had been left unextended to make it more cosy, so that the merest flick of her eyes, told Keely that Tarrant, directly opposite, was wearing a barely concealed smug look. Swine! she thought, knowing exactly what thoughts lay behind his smug expression. He knew as well as she did that Gerald hadn't stayed to be invited to dinner once he had seen her responding so fully to him in the garden.

'Gerald couldn't stay,' she explained. 'He has tickets for the theatre tonight. In point of fact,' she went on, just in case her mother was getting any ideas that she was romantically attached to Gerald, 'he only offered to give me a lift because he wanted to give his car a bit of a run.'

She weathered Lucas's dry look that said if she believed that, she would believe anything. But as her eyes could not help but catch the mocking gleam opposite that told her that in Tarrant Varley's view she would be lucky if Gerald offered to take her anywhere again, Keely was hard put to it to weather the storm of anger that took her.

'Is it likely that Gerald will want to give his car a run tomorrow, do you think?' asked Lucas, tongue in cheek as he went on to tease, 'Is he calling for you tomorrow?'

Keely managed to keep her smile in place. In normal circumstances, this sort of family teasing would have set the seal on her being accepted by Lucas, and as such would have pleased her enormously. But, with Tarrant about to do cartwheels at her expense, she was hating him afresh that he was taking even that pleasure from her.

She shook her head. 'I thought I'd catch an afternoon train,' she replied quietly—but only to have Lucas, his teasing manner falling from him, protest, 'Can't you stay later—for dinner? Catherine has so looked forward to ...' He broke off, a simple solution coming to him. 'Of course you must stay until after dinner tomorrow. Tarrant will give you a lift back to London.' He turned his glance to his son. 'Won't you, Tarrant?'

In the face of his father's point-blank question, there was little Tarrant could reply but, 'My pleasure.'

But that he had not tried to wriggle out of it did not make Keely feel any better disposed towards him. She hadn't missed that while Tarrant's mouth had been smiling as he had made his pleasure to give her a lift known, his eyes were glimmering with distaste at the thought of having to have her for a passenger. Well, he needn't worry, wild horses wouldn't have her a passenger in his car ever again!

'Oh, I couldn't put you to that trouble,' she thought she had better put everybody straight. 'Your flat is miles away from mine, and . . .' Her mother looking at her as though questioning how did she know where Tarrant's flat was made her break off.

Then all at once, beautifully, magically, as if the gods had suddenly decided that she should have that chance she yearned for to get even with Tarrant Varley, she saw that that chance was within her grasp—if only she had the nerve to take it! In a flash she was remembering how she had vowed to seize any opportunity 'with both hands'. She looked at him, and needed to receive no more than the icy blast from his steely look at her slip in letting out that she knew where his flat was to act on that vow. My God, she thought, had he been asking for it!

Not looking again at her mother, Keely made herself stay with those icy grey eyes as she resumed, her voice quiet, though loud enough for everyone to hear:

'. . . And you know, Tarrant, that the last time I was in your flat—you preferred me to stay the night rather than get your car out again to drive me home.'

'Keely!'

Her mother's shocked exclamation brought the colour to Keely's face. But nothing could take from her the feeling of triumph as Tarrant Varley, unable to deny a word she had said, in front of her very eyes went to look absolutely livid.

Though any apology she would have made for shocking her mother so; any explanation she might have wavered to make had she looked at her, went unheard as Lucas, his smile gone, asked, 'What are you saying, child?' his stern expression telling her that he was insisting that she answer.

'I . . .' she began, but only to be interrupted by her mother, Tarrant, she noted, had so far not said a word.

'I thought . . .' said Catherine, and broke off, a world of a mother's disappointment in her expression. 'Oh, Keely,' she went on sadly. 'You've always told me you would never give yourself until you fell in love.'

Half wishing she had kept her mouth shut, her feeling of triumph at having stirred Tarrant to impotent wrath not lasting long, Keely saw that her mother had clearly seen that no girl in her right mind would fall in love with Tarrant Varley. But, feeling decidedly ill at ease that her mother thought she had given herself to him without love, she caught Tarrant's impatient discrediting movement at the suggestion that he was the first man she had ever given herself to, that she was spurred into not regretting a thing.

She felt only hate then—and determination, as she thought, Oh, didn't he have it coming, then her eyes lowered lest anyone witnessed that hate, lest anyone saw the tremendous satisfaction she felt to be in a position to be able to set *him* up. Though Keely was hopeful that her mother would see the funny side of it later, when she answered softly:

'I *was*—keeping myself, Mother. I—meant to, honestly I did—only—only . . .'

'Good God!' exploded Lucas, saving her from having to go on. 'Are you saying that—that my son—*seduced* you?'

Remembering the way it had been, the way she had had no intention of responding, the way Tarrant Varley had had her responding to his kisses, any preconceived notions about keeping that girlhood promise to her mother so far forgotten that she would have willing been his, Keely could not in all honesty think what other name to call the way he had seduced her senses.

The nod of her head as, still keeping her eyes lowered—that memory of Tarrant's seduction of her for the moment leaving her speechless—was all Lucas waited to see.

'Is this true, Tarrant?' he demanded of his silent son. 'Did you house Keely under your roof all night?' And, determined to get at the truth, half hoping she was lying, Keely guessed, he went on sharply to ask, 'Did—did Keely spend the night in your bed?'

As that question left Lucas's lips, so she saw that she had had a good run for her money. Though a few short minutes of making that swine Tarrant Varley feel uncomfortable were, in her view, much too short. But, knowing that in defending himself to his father Tarrant would soon be telling him that though she had been willing he had not taken her, bravely she raised her eyes to look at him.

For long seconds she stared unblinking as she waited for the axe to fall. Waited again to know that her pathetic attempt to best him had fallen in the mire. But her eyes widened and she stared at him dumbstruck when, not attempting to defend himself, he looked from her to his parent.

'Yes, sir,' he answered, 'she did.'

Lucas's disappointment in him as he heard this confirmation was as great as her mother's disappointment in her, Keely knew. And it was touch and go then that she did not leap in and confess she had just been trying to get her own back on Tarrant.

But that feeling was very soon swallowed up, as hate in her reared when, his father taking him to task, she saw from a muscle that moved at the side of Tarrant's mouth that he was having a hard time not to burst out laughing at the absurd notion that she had been innocent before he had taken her to his bed, as angrily Lucas charged:

'Did it not occur to you that by doing what you did—that by taking this child's innocence . . .' he paused, and that was when Keely noted that Tarrant looked set to have a convulsion from the effort of holding in his derision, '. . . you stood to hurt not only Keely, but her mother too? And through Catherine—me?'

Keely saw Tarrant's eyes narrow as shortly he replied, 'It was not my intention to hurt you, sir.'

And that made her wildly furious. For from that terse statement, Tarrant Varley was making it plain that as far as he was concerned, while he did not want to hurt his father, her mother could go hang for all it would worry him. And nothing then would have stopped her from putting the boot in. Enraged, she hardly thought about what she was saying, before, only just managing to remember she had better stay demure and hide her flashing eyes, she was letting her voice be heard.

'It—wasn't all Tarrant's fault,' she said, keeping her eyes on her plate. 'We—discussed marriage,' she explained painfully. 'It was my mistake—I thought—I thought he meant to—marry me.'

The choking cough that came from Tarrant mingled with the gasp that came from Catherine, followed by her, 'Oh, my God!' But by then Keely was so hating Tarrant Varley and his insults to her and her mother that nothing would make her back down. Though she was careful that no one should see into her eyes—let those who would, think that it was embarrassment that kept her eyes glued to the tablecloth.

'You led this poor child to think you would marry her?' Lucas, the first to recover, asked his son sternly.

And Keely knew that the game was up. In no time flat Tarrant would be letting it be known that not only had she slept in his bed untouched, but that he would as soon consider marrying a barracuda.

But again she was to know surprise. For when Lucas was giving him all the time he needed to tell him differently, Tarrant was remaining obstinately silent.

'You had no intention when you took Keely to your bed of marrying her,' Lucas pressed, determined, it seemed, to have his son answer.

Keely knew then, no mistaking that Tarrant was angry, that it was only a matter of time before she was left with egg on her face. Though oddly, when, making no immediate reply, Tarrant at last answered his father, it was not to denounce her that he finally opened his mouth:

'I had no intention whatsoever of marrying her,' she heard him admit grimly.

'You had no . . .' As Lucas started to speak, so Keely thought she had been as brave as she could be expected to be.

'Excuse me,' she mumbled, and stood up, dabbing at her mouth with her napkin. Then, just as though to hear from Tarrant's own lips that now he had had his fun with her, she was discarded, and that he had no intention of marrying her was more than she could take, hastily Keely left the room.

Closing the door of her bedroom, she wondered if she should barricade herself in. She hadn't dared to look at Tarrant as she had left the table, but murder, she didn't doubt, was in the air.

It was with mixed feelings that she undressed and got into bed. That bond of closeness with her mother told her that first thing tomorrow would see her owning up to her. But, as a smile she couldn't help picked at the corners of her mouth, she was only human, wasn't she! For tonight, she hoped Lucas gave Tarrant hell. For if nothing else, she had again seen that Tarrant *was* honourable. Had he not been, he would have set them all straight before any of that hornets' nest downstairs had been stirred.

She smiled as she lay down and closed her eyes. It

had after all been lovely to see Tarrant Varley furious with impotent rage. What a gorgeous feeling it was to have her retribution and to know that, since he hadn't charged up the stairs after her to wring her neck, his sense of honour said he could do nothing but grin and bear it.

As she had gone to bed early the night before, Sunday morning saw Keely awake before seven and admitting to a feeling of guilt at the way she had dropped Tarrant Varley in it. Though as she remembered the way he had hardly been able to keep from bursting out laughing at any suggestion that she had retained her innocence, she found that feeling of guilt very easy to live with.

Nevertheless, the first thing she did, after taking a quick shower and pulling on some clothes, was to go in search of her mother. Confession time was at hand.

But on going downstairs and finding her mother making a pot of tea, she was soon to discover that whatever had gone on between the three she had left in the dining room last night, Lucas and Catherine must later have decided that whatever their respective offspring had got up to, they were not going to let it interfere with their newfound happiness.

'Smelled the teapot?' Catherine enquired when she saw her daughter standing in the doorway, her manner, to Keely's relief, not stiff as she had suspected it might be until she had explained, but warm and natural as it was most times.

'I thought you might be brewing up,' she replied, having the same weakness as her mother for an early morning cuppa.

'Lucas and I take it in turns to get up and take the tea back to bed at weekends,' said Catherine, getting out cups and saucers, and confiding, 'Though I usually end up joining him in the kitchen when it's his turn—it seems to take an age when you're waiting in bed for someone to bring you morning tea. Though you wouldn't know . . .'

She broke off, and Keely just knew, as her mother's eyes clouded over, that she had gone on to wonder if Tarrant had brought tea to her in his bed that morning after she had spent the night in his apartment.

'About last night,' Keely shot in hastily, 'I . . .'

'Not another word, Keely,' said Catherine, sharply for her, her disappointment pushed into the background as she told her, 'You're quite old enough to make your own decisions.'

'Yes, I know,' Keely replied, but wanting her mother to know everything. 'But what I said last night about . . .'

'Was more than enough,' she was cut off again, as Catherine, refusing to hear her out, went on, 'If you have any more to add—then I just don't want to hear it.'

'But, Mummy . . .' the name from her childhood slipped out. She didn't want her mother taking this remote stand. They had always shared everything.

'I should have guessed that something was between you and Tarrant when I saw the way he looks at you, the way you look at him,' continued Catherine as if she hadn't spoken, as she let Keely know that she must have seen the dagger looks flying backwards and forwards. 'But while it's instinctive in me to want to intercede—to be all on your side, I have Lucas to think of.'

And before Keely could interrupt to say that she knew and accepted that Lucas had to come first, Catherine was going on, just as though she had spent some hours getting it all clear in her mind:

'For all Lucas and I may appear old to you, our marriage is young. And that's a time when marriages can run into trouble if one isn't very careful.'

'You're—happy with Lucas?' asked Keely, swallowing hard on the appalling thought that when the question of was her mother happy had no need to be asked yesterday; today, through her trying to get back at Tarrant, that might no longer be the case.

'I've found joy with Lucas which I never found with your father,' Catherine answered her, the softening of her expression as she spoke her new husband's name sending Keely's fears that today was any different for them flying. 'I don't wish to malign your father,' she went on, coming away from her thoughts of Lucas to realise that she might inadvertently have hurt Keely if she was sensitive to her father's memory, 'But you know, I think, that he was not the easiest of men to live with.'

Yes, Keely thought, she had known that. But safe again in the knowledge that she had not wrecked the fragile beginning of her mother's new marriage, she could not resist wanting her not to be disappointed in her.

'But Tarrant . . .' she began, only to see that remote look come to her parent's face again as she said:

'No, Keely, I don't want to hear any more. You and I have never had any secrets, I know. But Tarrant is Lucas's son, and although he was blunt with him last night when he told him, beside other things, that he must keep away from your room while you're under this roof, Lucas loves his son as dearly as I love you.'

At last Keely saw the way it was. Lucas and Catherine must have decided that things were to go on as if that scene last night had never happened. Not only that, they must have decided that the subject was not to be discussed again.

She saw then that to insist on having her say would only have her mother feeling guilty and as though she was going against Lucas's wishes.

Not liking it very much, Keely realised, too, that she was only going to make matters worse, make it even more difficult for Catherine to take a middle line— favouring neither of the offspring—if she were to tell her that Tarrant had not touched her, that she had not given herself where love was not, simply because Tarrant had been convinced that she had wanted him to get her pregnant so that she could get her mercenary claws into him.

Feeling for the first time in her life that her mother had shut her out, Keely had to come swiftly to terms with the only important issue. Which was more important, a guilt-free conscience by unloading everything on to her mother—or her mother's happiness?

'So,' she said, a smile breaking so that Catherine would know she had accepted the way things were to be, 'what's for breakfast?'

Her mother laughed lightly, but Keely didn't miss the relief in her voice as she answered, 'You always were a glutton at breakfast time!'

She was not hungry, a slice of toast was all she consumed most mornings since they had gone their separate ways, but when the four of them later sat down to breakfast, Keely did her best to dispose of the bacon and eggs in front of her as though she was ravenous.

It had been in her mind to leave by the first train possible. But with Tarrant Varley sitting opposite as he had last night, the only word for the way he was deliberately ignoring her, grim, made her dig her heels in. She hadn't missed the searing look of hate in his eyes when he had come down to find her still in residence either.

So what if he did have more right to be at Inchbrook than she had? If he thought she was going to slink off rather than face him this morning, did he have another think coming! Oh, she was fully aware that underneath that polite 'Good morning, Catherine,' he had given her mother he was quietly seething. But he couldn't touch her, even if she did feel slightly scorched by that smouldering furnace of anger she had witnessed as his eyes pierced her when he had sat down.

Anyway, he needn't think anger was a one-way

traffic area, she was angry too. She wouldn't forget in a hurry the way he had told his father, 'I had no intention whatsoever of marrying her,' just as though he thought himself too good for her.

But angry with him as she was, by the time breakfast was over, having caught his narrowed eyed gaze on her a time or two, Keely was sorely in need of some fresh air. When Lucas mentioned that, as there was no delivery on Sundays, the newspapers had to be collected from the village, cheerfully she volunteered:

'I'll go.'

'Tarrant usually goes to stretch his legs,' Lucas replied.

But Keely was able to smile because she knew for a fact that Tarrant was not going to offer to go with her. 'His legs are older than mine,' she said brightly, her smile staying in place, although she did not miss the look which boded ill for her with which Tarrant greeted her remark.

He can't touch me, she repeated to herself as, down in the village, she paid for the papers and took them with her back to Inchbrook.

'I'll go and get some change,' said Lucas, and went off, despite her protest that it didn't matter about reimbursing her.

But she was to feel quite pale at the threat that was behind Tarrant's words, when he having no change either, he took his paper from her, his fury barely leashed as deliberately, his meaning having nothing to do with the money she had paid over, darkly he promised:

'I'll settle with you later!'

By the time lunch was over, Keely had had enough of Tarrant Varley and the suppressed violence in him. She knew by then that even if he was putting up a smoke screen of civility when anyone else was present, in his book they were nowhere near even. She had put his honour into disrepute with his father, and he, not having made any excuses for himself, was out to do her harm if he could. She just knew it!

To tell herself that she couldn't quite see what harm he could do her, because her mother's happiness was safe, and he was off to Australia for a month in the morning anyway, did not make Keely feel any more able to relax.

So it was that when lunch had been cleared away and they were all assembled in the drawing room, Tarrant hiding himself and his brooding silence behind a newspaper, Keely thought now was the time she had better light out.

'I'll just stay for a cup of tea,' she addressed her mother, 'then if you don't mind, I'll see about making tracks for London.'

'I thought I was taking you after dinner!'

Surprise kept Keely silent. She had thought Tarrant to be deeply immersed in his paper, but as that paper was lowered, she was to stare at the smiling mouth that had just protested that he was going to give her a lift after dinner. Though as she flicked her glance to his eyes, she saw no smile there—only a veritable volcano of rage was to be seen simmering in those dark grey depths!

'I should like you to stay to dinner, Keely,' said Catherine to throw her when Keely was still trying to recover from the molten aggression Tarrant's eyes were emitting.

'I—er—shouldn't want to put Tarrant to any—trouble,' she found herself replying, the look of him defeating her.

'It's no trouble,' he replied smoothly, his eyes showing, with both Catherine and Lucas now looking at him, nothing but a need to make amends if anything he had said or done had upset her. 'I give you my word,' he added softly, 'that I will take you straight to your flat.'

Not quite trusting him, she had never thought that he

might have plans to kidnap her anyway. But she did feel
a tinge relieved, she had to own, when Lucas spoke up
proudly on Tarrant's behalf.

'My son may have inadvertently misled you, Keely,'
he said, a strain of stiffness in his speech that told her
how much his pride in his son had been bruised. 'But he
never breaks his word, once given.'

Keely glanced at Catherine, and it was as she
recognised in her mother's expression a look that said,
'Forgive and forget, Keely—to please me,' that she saw
it was the least she owed her mother and her happiness
with Lucas.

Charmingly then, Keely smiled at the man waiting
to get on with reading his paper. 'Thank you,
Tarrant,' she said, and, smiling still, 'Your offer is
more than kind.'

She packed her case before dinner, wanting only the
sanctuary of her own flat. Though to be more precise,
she knew it was sanctuary away from Tarrant that she
wanted. For as the afternoon had worn on, she had
become uptight again when she remembered that with
Lucas saying that Tarrant never broke his word once
his word had been given, Tarrant had also given his
word that he would settle with her—and he had not
been meaning money when he had promised that!

On edge all through dinner, knowing it was
unavoidable that she must meet Tarrant's eyes some
time, Keely saw again, since she was the only one to see
it since she was sitting straight opposite him, that that
look of abiding fury was still there in his eyes.

And as the meal drew to a close she began to wonder
then that she had thanked him for his kind offer of a
lift. Was she, because of her guilt, imagining that he
had never looked at her that day without that hard glint
in his eyes that said, 'Just you wait, little lady'? Was it
only that because, like her, he was being on his best
behaviour in front of the newlyweds, he hadn't tackled
her to sort her out that day? Was he just biding his time

until there was no chance of them being overheard to give her a lashing frrom his tongue?

Keely made up her mind, as she went upstairs to get her case, that whatever Tarrant Varley had to say to her, it would be brief. When she said goodbye to him at the other end of their journey, she hoped that the journey would have been completed without either of them losing control of their tempers. But in any event, when she did say goodbye to him, it would be the shortest farewell ever recorded.

Strangely, though, having said goodbye to Lucas and Catherine, throughout that car ride to London Tarrant Varley had not one word to say. He must at some time have discovered where her flat was too, she guessed, for without so much as opening his mouth to ask, he pulled the Ferrari up outside the house where she had her flat.

Well, she wasn't going to hang around. If the searing glances he had been firing at her all day meant nothing more than that he was too furious to so much as lower himself to give her the ear singeing she guessed he thought she deserved, then she wasn't going to wait for him to drag himself to what he considered her level.

Without so much as a thank you, she turned smartly to get out of the car, and was pushing through the front door of the house before she heard his footsteps behind her.

In the hall she turned, quite ready, since neither parent was there to see, to slam the door in his face. Spotting her weekend case in his hand stopped her. So anxious had she been to see the last of him that she had completely forgotten that he had taken charge of her case at Inchbrook.

She held out her hand to take it from him—then discovered that when she had once sarcastically charged him with being a gentleman to the last, that was exactly what he was insisting on being. For he held on to her case, and having clung on to her dignity this far, Keely

saw that if that state was to be maintained, she would
perforce have to let him carry her case to her door.

Not giving him another look, she preceded him up
the flight of stairs to her flat and had the key in her
door when, taking his time, Tarrant had joined her.

'I'll take . . .' she began, breaking her silence as, her
door open, she held out her hand for her case—but she
never got to finish that sentence.

In amazement, she found that she was being pushed
physically into her sitting room, the door of her flat
closing with a determined snap behind him, as Tarrant
Varley came in with her.

'Who do . . .' she started another sentence which, as
alarm started to catapult through her, was destined
never to be finished either. For, scarcely believing her
eyes, she saw that he was slinging her case to a chair,
and panic gripped her by the throat as she saw the
jacket he had just shrugged out of swiftly follow it.

'What are you doing!' she squeaked, when, not
stopping at just shedding his jacket, the hard-eyed man
in front of her began unbuttoning his shirt.

'I congratulate you on the way you set me up, Keely,'
said Tarrant Varley coolly, only the blaze in his eyes
telling her that he was nowhere as cool as he was
sounding. 'The way you left me without an excuse, if I
wasn't to have my father think I was an even bigger
sinner than you made him believe, was quite masterly.'

'You had it coming,' she returned quickly, with some
vague thought that attack was the best method of
defence as Tarrant's fingers went to unbutton his shirt
cuffs.

'And now it's your turn,' he replied evenly, seeming
not to notice that her eyes were going huge to see that
his shirt had followed his jacket and that she was now
confronted by his broad naked chest.

'You . . .' she choked. 'I . . .' and, swallowing hard,
'What do you mean—it's *my* turn?'

Suddenly Tarrant had taken off the kid gloves, and it

was a snarling, aggressive man who was facing her as she backed away and he came after her.

'I took your virginity, did I, Keely?' he grated, not a glimmer of mercy in him as her face went white as he told her exactly what he did mean. 'By allowing my father to accept the implications you fed him, I've lied to him. But,' he snarled, 'only for a short while.' And as her back came up against a wall and she could not move any further, 'Soon,' he said savagely, 'though I'll have to overlook that I was not the first one to take your . . .' he spat the word, '. . . innocence—that lie will be the truth.'

'No!' Keely whispered, cowering back as, close enough to touch her, he reached out for her. 'No,' she choked again when, as though she was a feather weight, he picked her up in his arms. 'No!' she was still protesting when, either knowing the layout of many female apartments, or having an unerring instinct, he carried her to the bedroom.

But by the time he had closed the bedroom door, her instinct too had taken charge, and she was punching and kicking out wildly as she fought to be free. But wriggle and claw as she might, managing to get her feet to the floor as she did, she was to discover that, boiling with a waiting rage as he had been all day, Tarrant Varley was far too strong for her. And that she was on her feet, she was quickly to find, was only because he allowed it. And was only because he found it far easier to divest her of her clothing that way with his two hands free than by trying to achieve that same result while keeping one arm around her.

'No!' she gasped, shock taking her as her dress was torn away, her arms coming rapidly up to cover the front of her. But her action served only to bring more aggression roaring to the surface of her aggressor.

'Cut out the false modesty,' he grunted ruthlessly, a hand snaking out to grab her arm as, ignoring that she was trying to twist away from him, expertly he unhooked her bra and just as easily ignored the hot colour that stormed to her face.

But his glance at her breasts was no more than a cursory one. For in the next instant, aggression riding high, he had pulled her close, his bare chest burning into her breasts as he clamped his mouth hard over hers.

Her breath coming in short gasps, Keely managed to pull her mouth from his, and even succeeded in getting a kick in at his shin. But she had no time to feel satisfaction as her foot connected with bone, for the next instant she was thrown to the bed, her shoes speedily removed, so that any other attempt she might make to cripple him would prove ineffectual.

Making a desperate effort to scramble from the bed, she was thrown back on to her back before she could make it. It was then when Tarrant's hard body came over hers to keep her still as his hands got busy with the rest of her clothing—and his—that Keely started to feel real terror.

Renewed shock had her near to fainting as she felt his naked body lie over the top of hers. 'No!' she screamed, panic-stricken, praying that someone would hear her. But with televisions in the other flats blaring with the usual Sunday night viewing of cops and robbers with a plentiful supply of screaming police sirens, she had little hope of anyone coming to her rescue.

Roughly Tarrant gathered her to him. 'Scream away, darling,' he sneered. 'According to you, this isn't the first time I've had you.'

'You're—not—going to—have me—now,' she panted. But as he threw back his head, a dreadful cynical laugh leaving him, so a mighty fear hit her that she didn't have an earthly of stopping him.

'Don't bet on it,' he bit, his head coming nearer as she moved her head this way and that to avoid his kiss.

'I'll hate you for ever!' she cried, having fought hard, for the moment devoid of strength.

'You will when I've finished with you,' he threatened darkly. 'Forget all those other times men have had you and you've enjoyed it—this is going to be different. You've never had a man who hated you with everything in him while he was taking you, have you?'

'I've never had a man, full stop,' she rushed to tell him, with some forlorn hope that if she could get through to him, there might still be chance of a reprieve.

'In that case, sweetheart, you're never going to forget the first time,' he said harshly, clearly thinking her the biggest liar of all time. 'I'll see to that,' he promised.

His mouth descending brutally on hers effectually cut off any other attempt she would still have made to make him see that she was telling him the truth.

And with his lips on hers, his hands freely roving her body, his hands going where they would, Keely found renewed strength to fight him.

But for how long she fought him, pushed at hands that were caressing her thighs, searching, seeking hands, she had no idea. But Tarrant did not give up, and as the energy of passion in him grew stronger and stronger, so Keely was to feel the energy of her defence getting weaker and weaker.

Feeling drained of strength, in panic she found just sufficient strength to arch her body in a last attempt to throw him from her.

But the groan that left him told her that her action had only gone to incite him further, as that groan was followed by a jerky:

'You're not playing fair—this is supposed to be rape—you're not supposed to respond, to enjoy it.'

'I'm not enjoying it,' she cried, and was ready then to beg. 'Please, Tarrant,' she pleaded. 'Can't you see that what you're doing is wrong!'

'It feels right to me,' he answered humourlessly, and bent his head to roughly kiss her once more.

Defeated, knowing she could not fight any more,

weak tears welled to her eyes and rolled down her cheeks. Tears whose dampness he must have felt. For abruptly he took his mouth from hers. And as he stared into her tear-filled eyes, and as wordlessly she looked back, so for the first time did she see a hint of hesitation in him.

'Tears?' he questioned, his voice gone gravelly, doubt shadowing his eyes that her tears might be genuine.

She knew what he was really asking was, given her track record, what the hell had she got to cry about. Unspeaking, she shook her head, knowing by then that he was not about to start believing anything she told him at that stage.

'I—don't want you to—rape me,' she said with what voice she had.

'I never supposed you did,' he replied. And, his voice so low that she barely heard it, she thought she heard him add, 'It's not what I want either.' But whether it was what he wanted or whether it wasn't, his mouth was again descending on hers.

Though as if her tears had weakened some of that fierce aggression in him, little by little that harshness started to go from him. But quite when it was that his lips on hers turned to be gentle, giving, not taking, Keely was too used up then to know. But gradually, his hands stroking gently too, the panic that had been in her slowly began to quiet.

And as gently still Tarrant continued to stroke and caress her, his mouth moving to tenderly salute the pink tip of her breast, against her will Keely felt her body tuning to his touch. But that he was still with her, for all his manner of lovemaking had changed, told her that whether it was to be rape or not, Tarrant was determined to have her.

'Tarrant,' she choked, tears in her eyes still as he pulled back his head to look at her. 'Please—don't . . .'

'You're saying you don't want me?' he questioned, that tough aggression in him gone as he made her aware that he knew her body was responding to him, even if her head was telling her no, no, that this wasn't right. His head came nearer, his mouth again seeking hers. 'Would you have me lie to my father?' he asked. The next moment, his lips had met hers.

CHAPTER SIX

THE sound of a door quietly closing brought Keely awake. Dawn had broken, daylight showing up objects in the room which had been in darkness when Tarrant had been there.

To find that she had her bed to herself. To know then that the closing of that door signified that Tarrant had just left, brought the tears back. Burying her head in her pillow, Keely wept as in his arms she had wept.

Those tears were remembered, and she forgot nothing of how when their lovemaking had reached that fine peak where there was no turning back, as astounded shock had gripped him to discover that she was the virgin she had claimed, she had cried in fear that he would deny her need.

She had wept then as she had clung to him and begged him to stay, and had known, as a tortured groan had left him, that she would have her way.

And tears had stung her eyes again, this time from pain—pain that made her want to change her mind. But only until she had discovered such an unbelievable gentleness in Tarrant as he had soothed and held back on his own need, that it opened her mind to another discovery that was to see her clinging to him and never wanting to let him go.

In his arms afterwards, tears still wet on her cheeks, more tears had fallen. And Tarrant had remained gentle with her as with sensitive fingers he had brushed away her tears and told her, 'Don't cry little one,' and hushed her and, passion spent, had kissed her lips so tenderly and cradled her to him. And she had had to let him think that her wet eyes were because of what had happened between them. For, never more vulnerable, how could she tell him that her tears were from knowing that she had fallen in love with him?

To know that she did not hate him. To know that to repeatedly tell herself that she did was no more than a safety mechanism brought about by her subconscious which knew that Tarrant would never love her, had made it hard for her to stem her tears.

But the truth that Tarrant would never love her was no less painful in daylight than it had been in the darkness. In fact, with daylight, it was doubly brought home how little he cared. Had he any feeling for her at all save that innate kindness in him for any creature he had seen distressed, and he the cause, surely he would have stayed around to say—something?

That he had a plane to catch that morning and had probably hurried to his apartment to get his papers and passport together, and to pack, was irrelevant in her view. Only one fact stood out—Tarrant did not care for her and never would.

Mopping up fresh tears, Keely tried to find some stiffening to her battered feelings. But she could only thank God that Tarrant would be away for a month. For she knew it was going to take all that time for her to prepare herself to see him again, and with their family connection, she couldn't hope to avoid him for ever. But, as Keely got out of bed and bathed and got herself ready for work, it broke her heart to know that Tarrant had made love to her, not because he had any liking for her, or desire for her other than that all-male virile drive in him, but purely because he could not take it that the father he so respected should be lied to by him.

It was that thought, the thought that she just couldn't take knowing that Tarrant's only reason for taking her had been to square his consicience about lying to his father, that at last was to bring to her the stiffening she needed—that, or go under.

By nine that morning she was walking into her office,

a cold dead weight where her heart had been, so that
Gerald Cullen's look of reproach, the expression on his
face that said he looked ready to sulk for a week, did
not even impinge.

'Good morning, Gerald,' she greeted him coolly,
barely remembering that he had gone off in a huff on
Saturday after seeing her in a clinch with Tarrant.

'You do remember my name, then?' he queried
coldly.

'Will I ever forget it?' she answered sourly—and
didn't care a damn that he snapped at her to bring her
note pad in when she was ready, before he exited to his
own office and slammed the door.

Stowing her handbag, a tight control about her,
Keely opened a desk drawer and took out her note pad,
when the phone on her desk rang to delay her. She
picked it up.

'Mr Cullen's secretary,' she said into the mouth-
piece—and had tears in her eyes once more, shock
taking her to hear a voice she had not expected to hear
for another month.

'Keely, it's Tarrant,' he said, and paused. Keely did
nothing to fill that pause, she was too busy fighting
with all she had to remember that Tarrant had only
made love to her for his conscience's sake. 'I'm calling
from the airport.'

'So?' she replied shortly, and had to endure another
pause.

'So I'm ringing to say . . .'

'I'm just not interested in anything you have to say,'
Keely cut him off coldly, knowing that the man she
knew him to be was not the sort of man to take the cold
shoulder treatment without firing back.

Silence at the other end told her she should hang up.
But for the life of her, cold as she was being with him,
Keely could not be the one to sever this brief link with him.

'I—have to go,' he said at last, with a control over his
temper she could almost touch, 'I rang to . . .'

'Don't let me detain you,' said Keely freezingly. And with anger with him, with herself, with the whole world, washing over her, she put all the loathing she was capable of in her voice as she told him, 'As far as I'm concerned, if you went and never came back, you'd be doing me a favour!'

But if with those hating words her control had started to slip, then Tarrant's loss of control was not very far behind. 'You weren't saying that last night,' he reminded her acidly. 'Last night you were begging me to stay. Last . . .'

'And you—like the louse you are—did,' she cut him off.

Having slammed the phone down on him and his outrageous nerve in daring to remind her of how she had been last night—as if she would ever forget!—Keely was glad she had found the spirit to sever that link after all. But as tears threatened to choke her, how she wished that she hadn't. She wanted him, not just physically. She just wanted him, needed him, needed some personal contact with him. Oh God, no one had ever told her that love was like this.

She had wondered that her mother had not so much as given a hint that she had been falling in love with Lucas. But now Keely knew why Catherine had kept her growing love to herself. Love was such an all-consuming emotion. An emotion that had to be kept secret in that frailty of uncertainty in case even the merest whisper of a wrong word came to damage it. In her mother's case, the fear that a wrong word would take away the hope that Lucas might come to care for her.

Without hope herself, Keely wondered why Tarrant had bothered to ring. He had no need to remind her that he was going away—she had known that already. Colour was to flare to her face as later she was to come to the only conclusion possible. Tarrant had guessed she would be edgy with him the next time they met. He must have telephoned to tell her that since he would want to spend some time in his old home when he got back, would she kindly take advantage of the month he was absent by getting her visits to Inchbrook out of the way before he came home. Quite clearly, and this thought backed up the way he had left her flat before she had awakened, Tarrant Varley was saying that he didn't want to see her again!

Coming to terms with that fact had not been easy. But at the end of that first week which had seen Tarrant refusing to be ousted from her mind, Keely was no longer given to wanting to burst into tears at the drop of a hat.

By Friday, too, Gerald had come out of his sulks, and had relented so far as to ask if he could take her out to dinner on Saturday night.

'Can we make it some other time?' she asked, having nothing planned for Saturday, but just then preferring her own company.

'Got a date with Tarrant Varley, I suppose?' he asked humpishly, not being a man to take being turned down with a good grace.

'T-Tarrant's in Australia at the moment,' she told him—and was glad that that news pleased somebody, as Gerald's look lightened. Though whether he was in England or in Australia, Keely saw she had about the same chance of seeing Tarrant.

The second week of days stretching out endlessly finally drew to a close with Keely, having been telephoned by her mother on Thursday, promising to spend the weekend at Inchbrook.

She had told Gerald where she was going when he had again asked her out to dinner. But he had not this time volunteered to drive her. Though he had asked:

'Will Tarrant Varley be there?'

Keely had shrugged her shoulders, keeping her feelings well hidden. 'I shouldn't think so,' she had answered. 'He's not due back from Australia for ages yet.'

It was good to see her mother again. Good to see again the happiness that she and Lucas had found, even if it did take all her acting ability to put on a bright face and to keep cheerful that weekend.

Though if Lucas had heard from his son, Keely did not get to hear of it. For, knowing what had been said had gone on between her and Tarrant, it was as if Lucas thought it was more tactful not to mention him. And Keely's lips just would not frame the everyday question of 'Have you heard from Tarrant?' lest, having once pretended she had thought he was going to marry her, her question was seen as being put because she had more than a passing interest in him.

She felt better by the following Monday. Being forced to put on a cheerful face had made her feel more cheerful. Life went on, she had discovered. Even if you had an ache in you the size of which you could never hope to lose, life went on.

The Monday that saw the start of the fourth week since Tarrant had gone away started for Keely with the same forlorn hope that she would soon start forgetting about him. That night her mother rang asking her to come to Inchbrook that weekend.

'I can't put Gerald off any longer,' Keely replied off the top of her head. She had no idea exactly when Tarrant was returning, but if he turned up at Inchbrook over the weekend, then she did not want to be there.

'You're not serious about Gerald, then?' queried Catherine, and Keely guessed that her mother was wondering about her brief relationship with Tarrant, and if it had left any lasting effects on her.

'He's all right,' she replied, knowing because of the pact her mother and Lucas had made that Catherine would not pry into her feelings for Tarrant, 'but I haven't yet met the man whom I'm likely to settle down with.'

Keely had the same aversion to lying to her mother as Tarrant had to lying to his father. Yet she hoped what she had said conveyed that she hadn't yet met a man she had fallen in love with. Though what she had said was true at least, because the man she wanted would as soon go into orbit as settle down with her.

Feeling a little discomfited, she had said goodbye to Catherine, and resolved she would leave it a while before she telephoned Inchbrook. Her love for Tarrant was making it difficult for her to be open with her mother.

'Come out to dinner with me tonight,' said Gerald on Friday, and nearly gaped when without any more pressing, Keely answered:

'I don't mind if I do.'

But his pleasure was such that she was to feel guilt that through him she was salving her conscience that she had intimated to her mother that this weekend would see her not putting Gerald off any longer.

That was why Keely put herself out to be a pleasing companion to him that evening. But she was not sorry when she had said goodbye to him and was back at her flat. She was feeling tired, drained just recently, and guessed the mental torment of thinking so constantly of Tarrant must have taken over her physical energy as well.

She knew full well that it wasn't the mental strain of her job that was getting to her, because things were so slack at the office just now, usual at this time of the year, that Gerald had suggested it might be a good time for them both to take their annual holiday. Though since she had received an intimation that he would quite like it if she holidayed with him, she had changed the subject, and holidays were not referred to again.

Perhaps I need a holiday, though, she mused, as feeling tired enough to sleep for a week, she flopped into bed. Though what was the point of taking a holiday when she would still have no rest from thoughts of Tarrant?

To be rudely awakened the next morning by someone knocking at her door was not quite what Keely would have wished for her first chance of a lie-in since last Sunday.

The knocking came again, and it was while wondering why her neighbours couldn't drink their coffee black like she did when she ran out of milk that Keely pushed back the bedcovers and, still half asleep, dragged a robe around her to go and answer her door.

To come abruptly awake to see a tall, casually dressed Tarrant Varley standing there, brought the colour flaring to Keely's face, and had her staring at him speechlessly, a feeling of coming alive stirring in her as her heart started to race erratically.

That Tarrant appeared dumbstruck too, as, seeing her with her hair tousled from sleep, hot colour washing her, he looked back at her, was only a brief impression. Because then they were both moving at the same time, Keely going to slam the door in his face, Tarrant moving to step over her threshold.

His strength proved superior, and Keely, sickness grabbing at her stomach, went from a flushed pink to a sudden deathly white as he pushed the door wide, then closed it behind him. But his eyes were still on her, noting her sudden change of colour, and it was he who was the first to speak, as roughly he grated:

'Don't be alarmed. I haven't come for a repeat performance of what happened the last time I barged my way in here.'

Keely had not thought for a moment that he had. In fact as her stomach continued to churn and she knew that she was going to be sick, she wasn't thinking very clearly about anything as Tarrant went on to tell her:

'Your mother is ill—I thought you might want a lift down to see her.'

Feeling more colour drain from her face, promptly

Keely answered, 'Of course I want to see her,' as she tried to hold down the feeling of nausea that had her in its grip, while at the same time her mind became agitated that her mother was ill. 'What's wrong with her? Why didn't she—Lucas—anybody ring me to . . .'

'It's only 'flu,' soothed Tarrant quickly, seeing that her face had gone ashen.

'That can be serious sometimes,' snapped Keely, her thoughts panicky as she thought of how her father had started out with 'flu and had died. But she did not have time to say anything more. Needing the bathroom urgently, Keely had only just made it when the ghastly feeling in her insides waited no longer to be released.

That Tarrant had stared after her for only a moment before, on hearing her retching, he came to her aid, was an assistance she wanted to do without.

Sitting on the bathroom stool some time later, she wasn't sure that she didn't want to die that, having not seen her for a whole month, he should not only surprise her when her hair must look a mess, but that he had witnessed the indignity of her in the throes of vomiting. Not that it had thrown him. Deftly he had mopped her up, sponging her face and talking softly to her all the while.

'Feeling better?' he asked, when ten minutes had passed without her parting with anything else.

'I want to die,' moaned Keely, feeling as though she'd just spent half an hour being thrown around in a tumble-drier.

'You're looking better already,' he encouraged.

She didn't believe it—she still *felt* ghastly. But she was glad he was being kind. She was feeling too exhausted to find any return of acid had he been so minded.

'Come and take a comfortable chair in the sitting room. You'll feel much better there,' he coaxed.

Keely leaned weakly against him as with an arm around her he led her from the bathroom. Ensconced in an easy chair, Tarrant's arm no longer there, she leaned her head back and closed her eyes.

She heard sounds of clinking crockery in her tiny kitchenette, but had neither the energy nor the desire to go and investigate what Tarrant was up to.

When he came to push a cup of tea in her hands, having availed himself of a cup too, Keely felt it was just what the doctor ordered.

'Sorry about that,' she was able to apologise some minutes later when Tarrant had left her to drink her reviving tea in silence.

'Was it fear of me that triggered that off?' he asked tightly, his face gone grim as he leaned towards her. 'Or was it the news I gave you about Catherine that physically upset you?'

'Neither,' she answered, knowing that she was not afraid of him, only of herself. And she was able then to recall that she had started to feel queasy before her mother's name had been mentioned. 'More probably it was the fish I ate when I was out to dinner last night.'

'You were out to dinner last night?' he questioned. And just as though it had anything to do with him, shortly, he asked, 'Who with?'

Feeling better by the second, Keely started to feel niggled, as much by this sharp contrast in attitude from the kindness he had shown when helping her in the bathroom as anything else.

'Do I ask who you dined with last night?' she answered waspishly.

'No,' he agreed—then sent her a smile that nearly floored her. 'But if you did ask, I wouldn't baulk from telling you that she was a rather pretty blonde.' She felt ill again, though this time, as jealousy stormed in, Keely knew that it wasn't from any fish she had eaten. She saw Tarrant's grin widen, 'Well, a pretty blonde in a natty stewardess's uniform served me my dinner anyway,' he amended.

Relief from that green-eyed monster made Keely feel

better again. 'You flew in last night?' she enquired, a grin inside her as wide as the one he was showing.

'Quite late,' he replied. 'Though I was able to put through a call to Inchbrook before my father went to bed.'

'And he told you about my mother being ill?' She felt panic again as she wondered what she was doing sitting there when her mother was ill and needing her, and she did not wait for him to answer. 'I'll go and have a quick bath,' she said. 'Will you wait for me?'

Tarrant nodded. 'You'd better pack an overnight bag too,' he suggested mildly.

Keely hurried to do as he said, agitation growing in her that although Tarrant was sounding so calm, her mother must be really ill. Before he had gone to Australia he had been at pains to phone her to let her know he would be obliged if she would get her visits to Inchbrook out of the way before he returned—and that had to mean that he objected to having her under the roof of Inchbrook while he was there. To volunteer to give her a lift, to suggest she might stay the night, had to mean that her mother's condition was serious.

That this must be so was confirmed for her on the drive to Inchbrook, for never had she known Tarrant so amiable. Other drives she had taken with him had been completed in stony silence. But on this trip he chatted to her about everything under the sun, and she just knew it had to be that he was trying to keep her mind away from how gravely ill Catherine was.

But on arriving at Inchbrook, Keely was astonished to see that her mother was sitting out in the garden. That Catherine looked surprised, if delighted, to see her, was brushed aside by Keely as, hurrying up to her, she greeted her rapidly.

'Shouldn't you be in bed?'

'For a bit of a cold!' answered Catherine, blinking, apart from a reddened tip to her nose, looking the picture of health.

'Here's your case,' said Tarrant, distracting her as he pushed her weekend case into her hands. 'If you'd like to take it up to your room now, I'll rustle up some coffee for when you've unpacked.'

'Have the same room you had the last time,' murmured Catherine.

And, when it had not been her intention to leave her mother without finding out more about her condition, Keely felt Tarrant's hand at her back as he propelled her into the house.

That he was still with her and going up the stairs with her, had her halting halfway up the stairs. Though before she could voice the tart question of what the deuce did he mean by giving her the impression that her mother was at death's door, she again felt herself being propelled by him, further up the stairs this time, as he remarked:

'Your mother is really quite something, isn't she?' And while Keely was almost gasping at this turn-around, he was escorting her along the landing, and saying, 'Obviously my father was over-worried when he told me how ill she was. It doesn't look like 'flu to me. But then,' he added, 'Catherine isn't one to make heavy weather of illness, is she?'

'No, she isn't,' Keely replied, coming to a standstill outside the door of the room she had used on her two previous visits to Inchbrook. But she could not hold back from saying, 'You sound as though—as though you—admire her!'

Tarrant, his face unsmiling, met her eyes full on as quietly he owned, 'I do.'

Feeling as though she was floundering, her insides all of a flutter just from looking at him, she just could not let that statement go unchallenged.

'*You've* changed. At one time you thought . . .'

'I know what I thought,' he cut in. 'And I know what I did.' And his face unsmiling still, Keely's amazement was to grow, to hear him confess, 'I was wrong—

grievously wrong, I admit it.' And while she was only just this side of gaping, her mouth was to open in shock, as he went on, 'If it's any consolation to you, I have long since apologised to Catherine for the offence I caused by daring to offer her money. And,' he added, to have her staring at him stupefied, 'owned up to my father about that cheque.'

'You . . .' Rendered speechless, all Keely could think to ask, was, 'What did he say?' Only to have her heart go cavorting giddily, when Tarrant suddenly grinned and said:

'I have more respect for your pretty little ears than to repeat a word of it.' At that, as her mind went spinning back to how his lips had once sensuously played around her ears, Keely went pink. 'But the upshot of what he said,' Tarrant continued, 'was a threat to disinherit me.'

'He threatened to disinherit you!' she gasped, her mind rapidly brought back to hear that.

Tarrant's grin was still in evidence as he said, 'I told him I wouldn't blame him if he did.'

'But—he won't?' she questioned, having swung about herself. For at one time she would have thought, 'Serve you right!'

'I reckon I've made enough to survive even if he does,' said Tarrant, unconcerned at the prospect of losing his inheritance. 'Fancy a coffee?' he asked.

Keely opened the door of her room. 'Er—yes, please,' she answered.

But she was to find herself so stunned by Tarrant's changed attitude to her, that, unable to get over the way he had unbent to tell her what he had, she realised that every thought of her mother not being as ill as she had thought had gone from her mind, but she had unpacked her case and was on her way downstairs again, before it came to her that it had never been her intention to stay at Inchbrook that weekend!

Though with Tarrant having made the coffee and suggesting—and being backed up by Lucas—that

Catherine must rest this weekend while he and Keely did the cooking, the minute objection her self-preservation soul was trying to make that she should leave, and leave now, just had to be overcome.

How could she leave? she argued. Her mother did have a cold, and deserved to be cosseted a little. And anyhow, she just couldn't see Tarrant in the role of chef for the weekend—and they had to eat, didn't they?

With Tarrant peeling the vegetables, Keely went to town on the lunchtime meal. But with everyone tucking in at teatime, by the time it came to prepare the evening meal, everyone was groaning under the weight of Keely's conscience-salving determination that no one should die of malnutrition.

'Er—could we have a light dinner?' asked Catherine, owning to still feeling full from the teatime scones Keely had made, giving the impression she had only eaten a couple to please her.

'How about a cold meat salad?' Keely suggested, and guessed that Lucas was still full to the gunnels too when he promptly said he could think of nothing he would like better.

He seemed to enjoy his dinner too, she thought, but still insisting that Catherine did not do a stroke, both he and her mother were banished to the drawing room while she and Tarrant cleared away. Though knowing her mother well, she was privately of the opinion that they would be lucky to get away with trying to cosset her tomorrow. But Keely was glad she had stayed and had not rushed back to London as instinct had demanded.

She knew she was in a fool's paradise to have enjoyed her day so much. To feel so happy just to be near Tarrant. To have him this close as he bent near while helping her to stack the dishwasher—but she couldn't help it.

'That's the lot, I think,' he said as he straightened up, his grey eyes going to hers.

Her heart starting to behave peculiarly again that Tarrant seemed in no hurry to look away from her, Keely sought for something to say—and found it in a mundane:

'D-Do you think I should lay the table for breakfast?'

'I'll do it,' he answered firmly. 'You've done enough for today.'

'I've only ...' she started to say, only to be interrupted when, his eyes roving her face, he asked:

'Are you feeling all right now?' when she had forgotten that first thing that morning she had been upset by the fish she had eaten the night before. 'Perhaps you too should have rested,' he said, his very tone so regretful that Keely felt such a warmth for him she knew she was doing herself no favours by prolonging this time alone with him in the kitchen.

'Fish,' she said, and laughed, and wanted to go on laughing when his laughter joined hers. Oh, Tarrant, Tarrant, when you're this you, I love you so much, she wanted to tell him. 'I'm going to bed,' was what she actually said. And, too scared that he might see how it was with her, she did not even look at him to see how he took that announcement. 'Goodnight,' she said abruptly.

'Goodnight, Keely,' he answered quietly.

Having gone to bed early, to lie awake in the darkness and want to be back in the kitchen with this new friendly Tarrant, Keely knew she had been right to come to bed when she had. Never had she felt so close to giving herself away. One wrong word, that was all it would take, and Tarrant, as sharp as a tack, would know she was in love with him.

After what seemed like hours, she eventually fell asleep. But she was to spend a restless night, and awaken early. And, because she had missed her final warm drink of the night, she found that she was so longing for a cup of tea that it was impossible for her to go back to sleep again.

For a few minutes more she lay there thinking it was too early to get up, that her movements might be heard and that she stood to disturb the whole household. But when that longing for a drink of tea turned into a positive craving, Keely decided that she could be as quiet as a mouse, and that no one would hear her.

Throwing a robe on over her nightdress, stealthily she opened her door and tiptoed downstairs with never a sound. Though she was congratulating herself on how noiselessly she had reached the kitchen, on opening the kitchen door, an exclamation broke from her to see from the tall towelling-robed, bare-legged figure standing there. So at least one other person at Inchbrook was awake.

'I'm absolutely gasping for a cup of tea,' she said, feeling ridiculous as Tarrant turned and stared at her as though she was an apparition, too late now that her exclamation had alerted him that he had company for her to back out. 'Would you like one?' she asked.

'Couldn't you sleep?' he asked, idly leaning against the draining board as she filled the kettle at the sink.

Aware that with her scrubbed face and her all-over-the-place hair that she must look a mess, Keely went to stand the kettle to boil. But before she could answer him that it looked as though he couldn't sleep either—before she could so much as plug in the kettle—she was gripped by such a sudden and dreadful attack of nausea that the kettle went down with a thud.

Panic-stricken, she saw Tarrant's face showing instant concern as he saw her face go ashen and Keely looked feverishly from him. Then as her stomach insisted on no delay, and told her that there was no time to look for a suitable repository, she cried in a rush:

'I'm going to be sick!'

At once Tarrant had taken charge. 'Here,' he said, and the next instant Keely was bent over the sink, the cold tap running as she retched, retched and retched again, while Tarrant held her forehead and got over the surprise of seeing her one moment with a faint pink bloom of sleep on her skin, to the next moment being the ashen creature she now was.

'Oh God,' she groaned, weakness attacking her limbs, 'I feel awful!'

'Lean against me,' instructed Tarrant just as though he could see that her legs might fold at any moment.

Clutching on to him, she did his bidding. Leaning against him, she stayed by the sink until she felt her stomach would behave itself. But she was still feeling dreadful when she moved as though to say it was all over.

Wondering why it was that when she only ever wanted Tarrant to see her as beautiful as he had once implied he thought her, he should again witness her when she was at her worst, Keely was glad of the kitchen chair he pushed her down into.

'Must have been something I ate,' she said, trying to get over feeling so ghastly, trying to excuse the misfortune that seemed to be Tarrant's in that he was for ever mopping up after her.

'You ate only a light meal last night,' he commented.

And that made her feel snappy. For it seemed to her then, feeling washed out as she did, that he was accusing her of being sick on purpose.

'Well, I don't know what else it can be,' she said shortly, and found that even when feeling lousy, or maybe because of it, she still had sufficient spirit to lift her head to glare at him.

But Tarrant was not firing back at her. And the glare in her fizzled out as she saw that those grey eyes held a look that said that he didn't know what had caused her to be sick two mornings in succession either.

Then as she watched, just as though what he did not know had him searching and investigating until he did know, all at once she saw his brow shoot into his hairline, and as a look of being shaken rigid came over him, so she saw that he had lost some of his colour.

'What's wrong?' she quickly asked. Something had shaken him to his very roots, she knew it had!

But he was not answering. His eyes fixed on hers, Tarrant seemed speechless, so that, as dreadful as she was feeling, Keely very nearly left her chair to go to him.

'Tell me, Tarrant,' she said urgently, 'what's the matter?'

At that, at that urgency in her, Tarrant made a tremendous effort to shake off the shock that had taken him. He even smiled as he took a few steps and came over to her.

Quietly then, taking both her hands in his, that smile an encouraging smile now as he held her eyes with his, he said, 'Keely—my dear,' but he was to pause for a moment before he instructed, 'Now, don't panic—it obviously hasn't dawned on you yet, but . . .'

'But what?' she asked, impatient to know.

Something shattering had just occurred to him, she was sure of it. That quiet 'my dear' he had spoken warned her of it. For all there was a smile playing around his mouth, she just knew that he had some terrible news to impart.

But when, keeping tight hold of her hands, Tarrant did tell her what his thinking brain had brought him, Keely was to receive the biggest shock of her life.

'Keely,' he said, using her name as a softener, she was sure, 'I do believe—you are—pregnant.'

CHAPTER SEVEN

HER eyes gone enormous in her pale face, Keely stared at Tarrant in disbelief. Shock at what he had just said had her so near to fainting that she gripped hard on to the hands that were firmly holding hers.

'Pregnant!' she croaked, her mind in a ferment.

Recognising her shock, just as he recognised that since she was not hotly disputing his suggestion that it must mean he had hit on the truth, Tarrant's voice was quiet still, as he reminded her:

'You once told me that the women in your family had a long history of being sick from the word go.'

'Oh God,' Keely moaned, dazed, not wanting to face the awful truth. The truth that had her mind not been so full of Tarrant, she would have seen for herself. 'I—can't be,' she whispered, still trying to deny it, some contradicting notion in the far recesses of her mind telling her that it wasn't that easy to conceive, a wisp of memory being grabbed at of one woman she had once worked with who had had to try for ages to ...

'But you are—aren't you, Keely?' Tarrant breaking into her thoughts, his grey eyes pinning her as he refused to let her look away, making her face what she was trying to deny.

Panic starting to riot in her, she was made conscious that she had nodded her head when gently, she thought, thoroughly confused, his reply to her confirmation was to smile. Though what he thought there was to smile about, she did not know. As hysteria threatened, she felt more like screaming than smiling.

'I can't ...' she said, trying to hold down hysteria, but finding that she was too panicky to choose her words, as chokily, still trying to deny the existence of a child growing in her, she told him, 'I can't have this baby.'

Abruptly Tarrant's gentle manner left him, his smile disappearing with it. And she was seeing again a well remembered harsh, stern look on him that was sufficient to tell her that he had misunderstood her before he threw her hands from him, to tower over her as he roared:

'Don't you *dare think* of having an abortion!'

To discover what she should have been aware of before this, but hadn't, had been shock enough. To feel poleaxed now that she had that knowledge that she was pregnant, aside from the fact that she was still feeling grim from her sickness, was bad enough. But to have Tarrant bellowing at her when abortion had never been in her mind had the panic she was trying to keep down going wild.

'And don't you dare shout at me!' she yelled straight back, panic released in hot anger as she charged on aggressively. 'You've done enough as it is!'

Aggression met aggression head-on. 'Did you hear me?' he shouted, when she wouldn't have been surprised if they had heard him in the next village. 'I told you not to . . .'

'You don't have to tell me anything!' Keely shouted back. 'For your information—nothing was further from my mind!' she blazed.

But in having released some of her agitation in joining in a shouting match; while admitting to never having felt so mixed up as she did right then—not that she wondered at it in the circumstances—Keely was to feel perversity at work in her when she saw that Tarrant was looking at her as though he was not sure he could believe her. Well, she'd had it with him and his suspicious mind! If he didn't want to believe her, then she didn't see why she shouldn't give him something else to think about.

Seeing his smile nowhere about him now, as with

narrowed eyes he sternly studied her face, from somewhere Keely found a smile.

'Now why would I have an abortion, Tarrant?' she asked softly. 'Isn't this what I planned all along?' She ignored his impatient look. 'According to you I'd plotted within two minutes to present you with fatherhood.'

'Don't be stupid,' he rapped.

'Stupid?' Keely shook her head, her lips still smiling if her eyes were showing that she felt nowhere near like smiling. 'I think I've been very clever—I've got you just where I want you, Tarrant, haven't I?' she went on. But the smile was to die from her lips, as something inside her snapped. 'Or are you, as ever the honourable gentleman, now going to protest that you aren't the father?'

'Of course I'm the father!' he exploded. But she had needled him, and sarcasm was there, cutting through his anger as his voice quietened, and he said with that arrogance she remembered and hated, 'That is, unless you enjoyed your first experience so much that you've been practising with one of your fish-eating dinner companions.'

Keely had known that shock had taken her near to hysteria. But that Tarrant, even in anger, even needled by her as he had been, could, when she was still rocking from the news he had presented her with, say such a thing to her, had her beside herself with fury.

In an instant she was out of her chair, nausea ignored as the tension of the last ten minutes was released as she erupted. 'How *could* you!' she shrieked, only aware that she was hitting him when her small bunched fists came up against the hard muscle of his arms and shoulders. 'How could you say a thing like that!'

To find herself suddenly in those arms she had been pummelling, those arms firm about her, making it impossible for her to try to punch him again, made Keely feel all at once totally drained.

'That was a foul thing to have said,' Tarrant muttered, as weakly she leant against him. 'Forgive me,' he apologised, his hand coming up to stroke her hair.

Not expecting an answer, for long moments he held her, quiet now, against him, his hand soothing at the back of her head. Then his hands were coming to her arms, and he was moving her so that he could see into her face; her pale skin and huge eyes telling him all he needed to know.

'Without that shock I've just given you, you're still feeling rough, aren't you?' he asked kindly. And feeling spent, feeling that she was going to burst into tears at any moment, Keely could only nod. 'Why not go back to bed?' he suggested. And with that smile that weakened her so coming out to just about finish her off, 'I'll bring you up that cup of tea you were gasping for.'

As she pulled out of his arms, the thought of being back in bed had tremendous appeal. She moved to the door, but found that he was there to open it for her.

'I'll come with you,' he said. 'You look worn out.'

'I'd sooner have that cup of tea,' she told him, and insisted when he looked like arguing, 'I'll be all right on my own.' With those words echoing and re-echoing frighteningly in her head, 'I'll be all right on my own,' maybe because he could see that to argue would drain her further, he let her go.

Wearily she climbed into bed, and save for the fear that she was on her own in this, that she had to go through with it on her own, her senses were still too stunned then for her to begin to think about how she was going to cope.

Her mind in a turmoil, a blank black wall facing her, Keely felt panic again that her thoughts did not seem able to penetrate to the other side of that dark wall. And she was nowhere near to coming to terms with any of it when Tarrant, bearing her tray of tea, came into her room.

'Feeling any better?' he asked kindly, his aggression

gone as, putting down the tray, he came over to adjust her pillows so she should sit more comfortably.

I'm not an invalid, she wanted to tell him, but though physically feeling more settled, she was feeling as weak as an invalid from the storm of anxiety that was going on in her head.

'I'm—feeling more me now,' she replied, taking from him the cup of tea he handed her. 'Physically, at any rate.'

'But worried to death mentally,' he said, coming to perch himself on the side of her bed. 'There's no ...' he had started to say, his hand reaching out for hers on the coverlet, when a roar heard from the open doorway made him break off to hastily take the cup and saucer from her as she jumped, startled, her eyes going to see, before he could, who was the owner of that roar.

To see Lucas standing there, a look of fury on his face because, passing her door, he had seen Tarrant in her room clad only in his robe and holding her hand, made Keely try to snatch her hand back. But Tarrant was refusing to let her go, and the next moment, from nowhere, her mother had come to join Lucas.

Wanting to hide her head under the bedclothes as she saw her mother go to look as appalled as Lucas looked furious, and the two of them then moved into her room, Keely just knew then that one hell of a row was going to break out at any moment.

But as Lucas launched into an angry disapprobation that began with, 'I thought you'd given me your word never to enter ...' Keely was left dumbstruck to see Tarrant, still holding her hand, actually grin at his father, as he cut in:

'I know I'm forbidden Keely's room, Father, but I thought you'd be prepared to make an exception in this one instance of my bringing up an early morning cup of tea to my future bride.'

Sure she was going to faint, Keely found she was

again gripping on to Tarrant's hand as her mother exclaimed:

'Future *bride*!'

'Keely and I are soon to be married,' she heard him state. And while she just sat there completely shattered, she heard her mother accepting that lie, joy in her voice as she rushed over to kiss her, and Lucas went to shake Tarrant's hand.

It was about an hour later—her mother somehow gaining the impression that Keely was too excited to eat breakfast, and Tarrant, no doubt observing that his intended looked numbed, had suggested that she might like to have a lie in—that Keely, having had no chance to give thought to the baby she was to have, knew only one thing—she was not going to marry Tarrant Varley.

Physically, once she had had her bath and was dressed, she felt more her old self. But by then she knew with a certainty that somehow she had to stop this talk of a wedding before it went any further.

Her mother, she recalled, had been little short of ecstatic at the prospect of another Macfarlane becoming a Varley. Lucas too had shown himself delighted. As for Tarrant, he had shown that he wouldn't make a bad understudy for Laurence Olivier, with the way he had acted, for all the world as if he was a man who could not believe his good fortune.

That she wanted to marry Tarrant with such a yearning was the most difficult longing to deny. Had he loved her with a quarter of the love she felt for him, then all those dreadful things he had said in the past would be as nothing. But he had said those dreadful things. And he did not love her. And, in her heart, Keely knew that Tarrant did not want to marry her anyway.

Panicking again, a state she was beginning to wonder if she would ever be free of, she suddenly saw that she could no longer stay at Inchbrook. With both her mother and Lucas cock-a-hoop at the thought of her and Tarrant being married—soon, so he had said—she knew then that she had to get away. That they had to be told that there was to be no wedding, was clear. But, with Tarrant having the courage to confess to his father about the way he had insulted her mother, quite clearly Keely saw then that if she went downstairs now and told them that there was to be no wedding, Tarrant would not hesitate to tell them about the baby.

In five minutes, Keely had her weekend case packed and was leaving her room. Her mind by then was so agitated that she had no idea whether she was just going to slip off to the railway station and probably ring her mother from there to say she had remembered some urgent matter in London, or what she was going to do.

Her thoughts were all over the place as she started down the stairs. Had it been in her mind to creep off without seeing anyone, Keely was to find that that idea was wrecked before it was embarked upon. For as she neared the bottom tread, she was met by Tarrant.

At first she thought she espied a look of welcome in his face, but it was so brief as his eyes caught sight of the case in her hand that, facing the grim man in front of her, she knew it had only been her imagination.

'I'm just off,' she said, drawing level with him, to see and recognise that he had already gleaned that much for himself, and did not think too much of it. Though he was keeping any anger in him under tight control, she noted, when he remarked evenly:

' All right, I'll come with you.'

'No!' she said sharply. 'I'm going by train—alone.'

'And what do you suppose the parents will say about that?'

Attack, she thought, and was then fighting her way off the defensive. 'I don't particularly care what they think,' she tossed at him tartly.

'It hasn't occurred to you that they might think it a shade—odd—that my fiancée, new of this morning, has suddenly decided she would prefer to spend the day on her own?'

'I'm not your fiancée,' she flared, and feeling herself slipping into the defensive again, she found a touch of her old spirit to flash, 'It was you who told them we were to be married—it's up to you to tell them there's not going to be any wedding.'

'Oh, but there is,' Tarrant contradicted her in no uncertain terms. 'You're going to marry me, Keely Macfarlane, whether you like it or not.'

'Like hell I'll marry you!' she flared, panic clutching at her as she tried to sidle round him, only to find that he had taken a hold of her arm and was making her stay right where she was.

From the muscle that moved in his jaw, she knew that Tarrant was striving hard for control. But he was nowhere any nearer to letting her go, when he changed tack to get her to see reason, and stated tersely:

'I've accepted, taken as your word, Keely, that you will not think of getting rid of my child. But having accepted that, you surely can't expect me to accept that my son, should be born illegitimate.'

God, she thought, already in his mind the sex of the child she was carrying had been determined! 'Tough on you,' she snapped, that most peculiar perversity taking charge of her again, making her hope it was a girl child she was carrying.

She saw her reply had not gone any way towards cooling the heat of the fury in him. But, when his eyes were positively blazing, she was to witness that, albeit with a great deal of effort, Tarrant was still managing to maintain control of his temper.

'You're not well,' he told her shortly. 'You're not yet over the shock of discovering you're to have my child.' And his voice was gritty as he made no bones about telling her, 'But while I'm fully aware that you need time to adjust before you tell anyone about our child, make no mistake about it, Keely, unless you agree to smile prettily—agree to let me drive you back to London—then before the next ten minutes are up, I shall be telling your mother and my father—everything.'

'You wouldn't!' she gasped. But she knew very well that he would. From the harsh stance of him, she knew that if Catherine and Lucas thought him the biggest blackguard of all time—for he would not spare himself in the telling, she knew that—he would do exactly as he had said.

'Which is it to be?' he asked toughly.

The weakness of her love for him was to swamp her again before she replied. He was right, of course, she did need to make that big adjustment before anyone got to hear what had resulted from that night when she had thrilled to his lovemaking. But how could she, loving him as she did, allow him to leave himself wide open to some more furious wrath from the father he loved?

'Can we leave now?' she asked resignedly.

It was all the answer he needed to hear. Without another word he had taken from her the suitcase which yesterday he had considered not too heavy for her to carry, and with his hand still on her arm, he took her with him in search of Catherine and Lucas. And having found them, he lost no time in saying:

'Keely and I have ...' he paused to give Keely a smile, and seeing a threat in his eyes, she did her best to smile prettily back, 'have a lot to talk about,' he said with a grin. 'Have you any objection if we don't wait around for lunch?'

With a picture of her mother's smile beaming at her, and of Lucas's smirk which said that whatever they had to talk over, he knew it was more that the newly engaged couple preferred to be alone, Keely's departure from Inchbrook was achieved without any of the fuss that would have followed had it been on her own that she had gone to tell them that she was leaving.

On that drive back to London Tarrant had returned

to being the tight-lipped companion she knew of old, but to her way of thinking that was just as well. It was best for him to concentrate on his driving, for she knew that if he was still going to insist that she was going to marry him, then once they got started, there was going to be the mother and father of a row.

With the faint hope that perhaps it need not come to a row, that perhaps Tarrant had spent the time during the drive to her flat in seeing that marriage to her was just not on, Keely was out of the car in a flash when he drew to a halt.

'Thanks for the lift,' she threw over her shoulder. But she knew she was on a loser when, giving her a menacing look, Tarrant, her case in his hand, was out of the car and impatiently opening the front door and waiting for her to go through.

'There was no need for you to bring my case up,' she said, still hoping he would see that they had nothing to discuss as he went with her up the stairs and into her flat. 'I could have carried it myself,' she added, knowing she was talking for the sake of talking. Nerves were grabbing at her as she saw that, again keeping his temper in check, there was a tough look about Tarrant that told her never did he not get his own way when once he had made up his mind to it.

Well, in this instance, she thought, that same determination about her, as placing her case down Tarrant straightened to face her, he would jolly well have to back down. She was not going to marry him, and that was that.

But his arrogance was to leave her winded, when without preamble, in a voice that brooked no refusal, he stated, rather than asked:

'I suggest a special licence. I'll attend to it first thing tomorrow. We can be married before the week is . . .'

'Now just a minute!' That he did not care to be interrupted, that he did not at all like to have her butting in when he was imparting the facts of the plan he had formulated, was apparent as darkly his brow came down. But that didn't worry Keely as, furious that he thought he could calmly tell her what *they* were going to do, and expect her to go meekly along with it, she charged on to put him straight. 'In case it has passed your notice, I'll repeat. I am *not* going to marry you.'

'Of course you are,' he rapped, a master, she saw, in brushing aside what he thought small insignificant objections. 'I don't know the procedure yet, but all being well, we should be able to have the ceremony on Thursday.'

Her anger spiralling that she seemed to be talking to a brick wall, Keely was in fast to flare, 'There is *not* going to be any ceremony!' And before he could again try to override her, as looked likely from his impatient movement, she was in there smartly to tell him, 'There is no way I am going to marry you, Tarrant Varley,' racing on when she saw he was about to get in, 'I'm not having you, in years to come, telling me that I tricked you into marriage!'

She saw that muscle move in his jaw that had told her before that he was having a hard time with his self-control. But, expecting him to come slamming back at her, she heard he had controlled that urge.

'I expect I deserve that comment from remarks I made before I knew you,' he said curtly. 'But,' he went on to let her know what he thought of her comment, 'should I at any time be such a lout as to throw such an accusation at the mother of my child, then you have full knowledge that such an accusation wouldn't stand up.'

'Why wouldn't it?' she found herself arguing, when all she wanted him to do was to accept that she wasn't going to marry him, and then go.

'You have a short memory, Keely,' he told her—and succeeded in making her go scarlet when, without any sign of embarrassment himself that she could see, he went on to remind her, 'If you cast your mind back to that night I determined to have you,' her sudden high colour told him she had forgotten nothing, 'you will recall,' he continued, 'that you did not trick me into your bed. That you,' he pressed on, 'fought valiantly to *prevent* me from making love to you.'

In the midst of coping with the memory of how gently he had made love to her; how afterwards, as if she was some wounded creature, he had cradled her tenderly until she had fallen asleep, Keely was to experience the oddest of sensations. Never had she expected to feel maternal, but as the first sensation of protectiveness to her unborn child stirred in her, she was fairly hurling at Tarrant:

'My child was not conceived from rape!' a hostile repugnance in her that he was daring to suggest that it had been.

'Neither it was,' he agreed, a softening taking the hard edge off the way he had been with her, as silkily he added, 'Your chemistry betrayed you, didn't it, Keely?'

She wanted her anger back, needed to be tough to answer him. She did not want him flushing out that weakness in her as he reminded her of how it had been. Of how he had stirred her to such a pitch, by then knowing herself in love with him, she had freely given of herself. But it was to be pride that Tarrant unleashed in her when, waiting no longer for her to reply, coolly, his eyes watching her closely, he went on to state:

'But—love—wasn't there either, was it?'

The weakness he had wreaked in her abruptly vanished. Plainly he was telling her that he had no love for her. But—God, was he suspecting that she loved him! It seemed of paramount importance just then to put him doubly right on that score.

'No,' she replied woodenly, 'love was not there.' And pride digging in when this time he had nothing to answer, pride that had been hurt that he had found it necessary to let her know that he could never love her, stopped Keely caring then what she told him so long as

he got the message that he was the last man she would
not only find it impossible to love, but also that he was
the last man she would think of marrying.

'We've rather drifted away from the subject, haven't
we, Tarrant,' she said as coolly as she was able. And,
going straight to it, 'But you can forget any *honourable*
intentions you have towards taking responsibility for
my child . . .'

'Our child,' he broke in tersely, aggression in him
starting to break that she was trying to cut him out. 'I
intend to see to it . . .'

Shaking her head, her attitude as lofty as his, as
pride, having surfaced, refused to disappear in a hurry,
'Forgive me Tarrant,' she said insolently, her nails
digging into her palms as she forced herself to go on,
'but who gave you the right to think that you're the
only affluent male I know who would be prepared to
make my baby legitimate?'

As soon as the words were out, Keely knew she had
gone too far. He had had a hard time keeping his
temper in check before. But at her implication that she
could quite easily get some other well-heeled man she
had more liking for to take over his responsibility,
Keely saw a towering rage take him.

She wasn't quick enough in backing away. For like
lightning, looking as though he was going to hit her,
Tarrant had covered the space between them, and his
hand had indeed left his side, before some superhuman
control stopped him. In a white-hot fury, then it was as
his face paled to know he had been within an ace of
striking her, that, his control iron-hard about him,
Keely heard what she had wanted to hear all along.

'My God!' came through his clenched teeth, as he
turned rapidly from her and went towards the door as
though in need to be away and quickly while he still
had his rage in check. 'I'm going,' he said jerkily,
'before for the first time in my life, I strike a woman.'

Staring at him, her panic that he had been going to

beat her black and blue for what she had said subsiding, but scared still, Keely found her pride would not let her lie down.

'And a pregnant one at that,' she found the spirit to jibe.

But as he checked a movement back to where she stood, she saw that in jibing at him when he was already fighting for control, she was tipping him over the edge! And she knew then, as his face went paper-white, the raging torrent of his fury barely reined, that just one more word out of her and she might yet feel him setting about her.

Too scared of the suppressed violence in him to so much as blink, her throat became a desert when, meaning every word, his hand on the handle of the door, Tarrant had her going as white as him when he ground out the words:

'Just mark this, Keely Macfarlane, and mark it well. You just so much as *think* of marrying anyone but me—and I'll kill you!'

CHAPTER EIGHT

To be more severely indisposed than ever the following morning was the only respite Keely's mind had from Tarrant since, in a thundering rage, he had left her flat yesterday.

With her mind on the ghastly time she had in front of her if each new morning saw a further increase in her sickness, she staggered totally debilitated from the bathroom. How desperately her mother must have wanted her baby, that she had welcomed feeling like this, she couldn't help thinking as she collapsed into a chair.

Eventually she started to feel better, but even knowing she was going to be late for work, she still felt too exhausted to bathe and dress. She had better put her alarm on to wake her earlier tomorrow, she thought tiredly, for if this was the way it was going to be, there was no way she could rush around to try and catch up on lost time.

At last, still feeling shaky, Keely made it to her office. But she was in no mood to placate Gerald, or his jealousy, when, ignoring her apology for being late, he told her grumpily:

'Tarrant Varley's been on the phone for you.'

Disregarding that Gerald seemed to think he was owed any explanation that Tarrant had telephoned to speak with her, quietly Keely put her shoulder bag away.

'Did he say what he wanted?' she asked. She was glad she had not been there, but she could not help wondering how her heart could find the energy to hurry up its beat just on hearing his name, when, if he was still going to insist that she marry him, she would need

more energy than she had just then to fight him. 'I'm
not the message taker,' replied Gerald stuffily. And as
Keely thought, Oh God, men! he turned about and
went into his own office, letting her know he was out of
sorts by closing the door between them.

She took some work from her desk drawer, but her
mind was only half on what she was doing, her
thoughts drifting back to the mammoth rage Tarrant
had been in yesterday, and how she had still been
trembling from the barely leashed violence in him ten
minutes after he had gone.

Not that she was going to marry him. He didn't want
her, didn't care about her. All he was concerned about
was that no other man should play father to his child.
And that was the only reason he had become so
enraged—she had infuriated him with her intimation
that she could easily get some other man to give his
flesh and blood a name.

It was a common occurrence for the phone on her
desk to ring, but when she had been at work for not
more than five minutes and it suddenly pealed for
attention, Keely nearly jumped out of her skin.

She knew then that if she wasn't to end up a nervous
wreck, she was going to have to do something about it.
Though to pick up the receiver and hear Tarrant's voice
as he told her that he had rung her flat but must have
missed her, was not at all conducive in getting her
nerves together. Nor was it any help to remember that
he had also rung the office before she had got there,
that recollection bringing with it as it did a suffocating
feeling that Tarrant was hell bent on hounding her until
she agreed to marry him.

'What do you want?' she asked disagreeably.

'You know what I want,' he replied, sounding tough.
'I shall have what I want too.'

Like hell you will, she thought. But she was glad to
find that the spirit in her that had lain buried all
morning was beginning to stir.

But, when she had nothing to reply and the pause lengthened, she found she could not be first to put the phone down. Then she found that, presumably having thought he had waited long enough, Tarrant was not putting the phone down either. Though that aggression she had heard in his voice had gone when, quite kindly, he asked:

'Was it bad this morning?'

She did not pretend not to know what he was talking about. 'Remember yesterday morning—double it,' she said sourly, not seeing why he shouldn't know. In her view it was most unfair that, since half the responsibility was his, he couldn't take a turn to have an early morning rush for the bathroom.

'Poor Keely,' he sympathised, his tone weakening her, bringing tears to her eyes. Though not for long, as he promptly got her back up by taking charge and telling her, 'You can't go on like this. I'll make an appointment for you to see a specialist. Most likely he'll be able to give you . . .'

'Thank you, but no,' she cut him off. 'I'm quite able to make my own decisions—quite able to take care of myself.'

'There's no need for that,' he came back, a sharpness in his tone. 'From now on that's my job.' And coming over all authoritarian and not endearing himself to her in her present mood, he went on to order her about, which did not sit at all well with her. 'And talking of jobs, there's no need for you to drag yourself to that office every morning. Go now and tell Cullen that you're leaving.'

'Who do you think . . .! I'll do nothing of the sort,' Keely told him shortly.

'You want me to come over and tell him for you?'

'No, I don't!' she hissed, only just remembering that Gerald was in the next office and might hear her through the thin walls and come to investigate if she did as she felt and started yelling. 'Don't you dare step one foot inside this building,' she seethed, panic gripping her that he was just as likely to ignore anything she said. 'If you come anywhere near Cullen's I swear I'll never speak to you again!'

'So you do intend to speak to me again,' he took up. 'Well, that's a beginning. From there we . . .'

'Goodbye, Tarrant,' said Keely coldly. Far from there being any beginning with them, this, to her thinking, was where it all had to end.

'I haven't finished,' he retorted toughly.

'Yes, you have,' she snapped back.

But she still had not put down the phone when, his voice authoritative again, he instructed sharply, 'Put me through to Cullen.'

'No,' she said point blank, not trusting him an inch.

But she was then to hear that Tarrant was suddenly all the high-powered business man. For curtly he rapped down the phone.

'Look here, Keely Macfarlane, I haven't any time to waste. I'm up to my eyes in it today catching up on a backlog of work that was waiting for me.' Only then did she recall that this was his first day back at work after a month spent in Australia. 'And though it may have escaped your notice that Varleys sometimes do business with Cullens, I need to speak with him on a business matter.'

His tone was such that she almost put him through without another word. But as her hand went to the button, she remembered that business or no business, this was the first time that the head of Varley's had rung personally to speak with her employer. She recalled, too, that if Tarrant had wanted a business word with Gerald, he had had the opportunity when he had telephoned earlier—though of course he might not then have had his papers sorted out. But she was still hesitating to jump to his bidding when she thought how all of a sudden Tarrant had changed from being a man who had been ready to take time out to come and hand in her resignation for her, to being a man who now did not have a minute to spare in his crowded day.

'You're not going over my head to tell him . . .' she started to question, but all that was coming from the other end was a terse silence. 'You won't say anything about . . .' She broke off, fear that he was going to tell Gerald about the baby mixing with uncertainty that she might in actual fact be going beyond the demands of a secretary's job and blocking what could be an important business call. 'Tarrant,' she said, when having issued his orders he seemed to have no intention of saying anything else, she remembered Lucas saying that his son never broke his word. 'Tarrant, will you promise me that if I put you through, you won't say anything that will lose me my job?'

For a moment she thought the only answer she was going to get would be a barked out order not to waste his time but to connect him immediately. But it was only silence she was to hear for a few more seconds, then:

'Your work means that much to you?'

Keely liked the work she did, but she was certain of one thing—that she was not going to marry Tarrant, nor was she going to take a penny from him—so now more than ever did she need a job that paid well. Circumstances decreed that it had to be more the money the job brought that meant a lot to her, than the luxury of job satisfaction.

'Yes,' she said quietly, 'it means a lot to me.'

How Tarrant took her answer she had no way of knowing. Whether he thought that perhaps she was more interested in Gerald than her job, she could not tell, because after a pause, his voice was there again to agree coolly:

'Very well. Now put me through.'

In no time at all Tarrant had, it seemed, completed his discussion on the business matter he had needed to speak to Gerald about. And before Keely was anywhere near to finding an answer to—had she been right to take that 'Very well' as a promise that he would say nothing to her employer—Gerald himself was coming from his office, his expression one of concern as he peered closely at her.

But he was to have her hating Tarrant Varley with all she had for a few moments when, his scrutiny of her pale face finished with, he said kindly:

'Get your coat on, Keely.'

The swine! she thought, instantly furious. That 'Very well' had not been a promise at all! 'Why?' she asked Gerald, having no intention of going anywhere.

'You're too loyal, my dear,' smiled her employer regretfully, 'and it's all my fault.'

Wondering what he was talking about, she stared at him, her thoughts momentarily off Tarrant, as she asked, 'What's—your fault?'

When she hadn't moved, it was Gerald who took her jacket from the coat stand. 'Tarrant Varley has just told me how he had to take you down to Inchbrook for your mother to look after you because you were so ill after eating that fish on Friday,' he said to her amazement as he handed her her jacket. 'He also told me that you insisted, even though you were far from well, on being brought back last night so that you could come to work today.' He smiled again that she appeared to be surprised that he knew so much. 'I blame myself,' he went on, his smile fading. 'But as I've just told him, that fish restaurant I took you to had been well recommended—but it makes me feel terrible that through me you've been so ill.'

To have Gerald insist that he drive her home, when in truth she was starting to feel so much better, was something Keely had no option about. Apologising all the way now that he knew from Tarrant Varley that she was still feeling rough, realising only as she spoke to him that his earlier phone call had been purely to enquire how she was, Gerald would have stayed to tuck her up in her bed, had she let him.

'Are you sure you'll be all right now?' he insisted, making her feel a fraud for feeling better and better by the minute. 'Would you like me to drive you down to your mother?' he asked, as he looked at her anxiously.

'I'm fine, Gerald, honestly,' she protested, and knew he didn't believe her when he patted her hand and instructed:

'Now you get into bed the minute I've gone. And don't think of showing your face inside the office until you're really better.'

Bed was far from her mind when Gerald, having shown a lovely side to his nature in the shape of his concern and kindness, had gone. She felt guilty that, suddenly feeling perfectly fit, she had almost a whole day off work for nothing.

The trouble was, she was to think an hour later, having made herself a cup of coffee and tried to concentrate on reading the paper, that needing the same action which yesterday had seen her clearing up all outstanding jobs, she had nothing to do that left her with too much time in which to think.

Yet no matter how hard she tried, she was finding it impossible to eject thoughts of Tarrant from her mind. It was desperation in the end that when, having to have some activity of some kind, Keely moved on the impulse to switch her furniture around.

Some of her furniture was of fine quality, having come from her old home, so she was careful not to scratch any of the one or two heavy pieces. Though since she had had a change around a couple of times before, she had just about got the knack now of how it was done.

The last piece in place, she looked round to realise that she preferred it the way it had been before, and had just decided that she must be thoroughly mixed up inside not to have envisaged in advance that the sideboard had never been meant to go under that window, when the phone rang.

Immediately, all thought of first having something to eat and then changing the furniture back again left her.

Her insides were all of a flutter as she realised that since no one but Tarrant and Gerald knew that she was not at the office, it could well be Tarrant! Gerald, she was fairly sure, would not ring to fetch her from her bed to answer the phone, when he had been so concerned that that was where she headed the moment he had left.

Desperately trying to ignore the persistent ringing, she realised suddenly that her mother might have taken it into her head to make one of her rare telephone calls to her place of work. The thought of her ensuing bewilderment to hear from Gerald how her daughter had been so ill at the weekend that Tarrant had taken her to Inchbrook to be looked after was sufficient to have Keely nervously picking up the phone.

'Were you having a lie down?'

To hear Tarrant's voice, to know that her first guess had been correct, brought back that same suffocating feeling of being hounded that she had felt in the office. Only this time, it was to be felt more acutely.

'It would be just the same if I was,' she said irritably.

'You can go and put your feet up the minute I'm through,' said Tarrant, strangely not rising to her irritation. 'It occurred to me that I'd better ring to tell you not to make any other plans for tonight. You and I have to talk, Keely—I'll come round.'

'Save yourself a journey,' she snapped, and, feeling she was being driven into a corner, her palms starting to sweat, in a sudden panic, she did no more than slam down the receiver.

For the next two minutes, in panic, her mind without controlled thought, Keely's thoughts were darting to wonder if feelings of panic were something that affected all newly pregnant women.

But, making herself sit down, making herself attempt some rational thought—she knew only that she felt trapped; her flat was far too accessible.

I've got to get away, she thought, a terrible feeling that if she did not, the pressure Tarrant was keeping up would see her weakening—giving in. Would see her agreeing to marry him when she knew full well that the only sort of marriage it would be was a duty marriage.

Acting on impulse agitated lest Tarrant, however busy his day was, would forget he had told her she could go and put her feet up and might at any second come knocking at her door, Keely went over to the phone. Her words unplanned, in no time she was speaking to Gerald, reminding him of how slack things were at the moment, and telling him she felt in need of her holiday now.

'One week, do you mean?' he asked, going on kindly, 'There's no need to take sick leave out of your holiday allowance. Take the rest of the week off—I'll see you next Monday.'

In her agitated state, Keely was of the opinion that a month wouldn't be long enough to sort herself out. 'I'd rather have two weeks, Gerald,' she compromised. 'And I really would prefer to take it out of my holiday allowance.'

That Gerald's show of kindness had worn rather thin that she was insisting on two weeks' as reluctantly he agreed, barely touched her.

No sooner had she put the phone down than she was haring around throwing things inside a suitcase. Still with no clear idea of where she was going, she was almost out of the door when it occurred to her that since she wanted to be incommunicado for the next couple of weeks, her mother would be worried to death if she didn't warn her not to expect to hear from her.

Again she picked up the phone to dial, in such panic Tarrant might arrive at any moment that she could sort out any feasible reason why she, supposedly newly engaged to Tarrant, was taking a holiday on her own somewhere.

But, as luck would have it, neither her mother nor Lucas was in when the phone at Inchbrook was answered. And having said who she was, she heard one of the day staff telling her that Mr and Mrs Varley had taken advantage of the weather to go for a picnic lunch, adding, 'I'll be pleased to give Mrs Varley a message if you would care to leave one.'

'Would you tell my mother that—that, as things are slack at the office, I'm taking two weeks' holiday, but that I'll ring her as soon as I get back?'

Assured that her message would be passed on, Keely lost no further time in locking up her flat, and lugging her suitcase with her until she found a taxi. Only when she was safely inside the taxi and on her way to the railway station did her feeling of panic begin to let up. Running away it might be, but she knew she had made the right decision.

It was to the seaside town of Folkestone that Keely had bolted. But it might have been anywhere, for all the notice she took of her surroundings. And it was a week the following Wednesday, when her two weeks were nearly up, that, having been aware for the last nine days that her flight from Tarrant had been totally unnecessary, a thoroughly depressed Keely was giving thoughts to her return.

She would have to contact Tarrant to let him know as soon as she got back—she knew that. She had in fact thought of writing to him to let him know that way, for know he had to.

But when on the first night of her panicking departure from London she had learned that there would be no baby, she had been hit by such a feeling of despondency that she could not so much as think of not having her baby, much less put down on paper that she had miscarried.

She had tried hard ever since to lift her defeated spirits, tried hard to think that it was all for the best. But to tell herself that she was being unreasonable, irrational, not to say downright ridiculous to want the baby she had lost, was of no help in shifting the weight of melancholy.

It was no use either, she found, to tell herself that she had probably never been pregnant in the first place. That after all, it had never been medically confirmed. Because she just knew that she had been carrying Tarrant's child—with or without that dreadful sickness, she just knew.

That Tarrant would be clapping his hands, and most likely jumping through hoops to know that he need no longer feel honour bound to marry her, gave her little comfort. At least he would cease hounding her, she thought, trying to look on the bright side. But even that thought made her want to burst into tears.

That night she went to see the busy proprietress of the clean and homely boarding house she had booked into. 'I shall be leaving tomorrow, Mrs Miller,' she told her, thinking she might just as well be fed up in her flat as in Folkestone.

'Not staying until Saturday?' queried Mrs Miller. Then with a motherly look, 'Got some nice man waiting for you?'

Keely smiled because it was expected of her, and agreed that she had, then returned to her room to pack. Was Tarrant nice? Remembering the way he had held her tenderly in his arms that time, she rather thought that—when he managed to forget his aggression—he was. The trouble was, when he heard what she had to tell him, she could cancel out that he was in any way waiting for her.

She was glad to get back to her flat, even if more guilt, and she had gone through plenty of that in Folkestone, awaited when she saw the new arrangement of her furniture.

Oh, what a fool she had been! She should have realised, knowing her family history as she did, how easy it might be for her to miscarry.

The trouble was that, never having been pregnant before, knowing nothing about it apart from the technicalities she realised now that she should have seen that bumping heavy furniture around was something to be avoided. That she had heaved her furniture around several times before without feeling any ill effect was no excuse, because she had not been pregnant those other times.

She felt a pang of guilt as she realised that what she had to tell Tarrant must be said over the telephone, since she just could not bear to see the truth of her stupidity written in black and white; and she fought for courage to lift up the phone to get it over with.

Still not sure she might not break down since those words had to be said, not written, the phone at last in her hand, Keely dialled Varley Industries.

Almost immediately her call was being answered, and she was off to a stammering start, as she asked, 'C-can I—speak to Mr Varley, please?'

Guilt clouded her mind as she waited to be put through. Guilt that when she had given little thought to the life growing in her, it was not until that child was no longer there that she had seen how fiercely she had wanted Tarrant's child.

'Mr Varley's secretary, can I help you?' said the secretary she had met on one never-to-be-forgotten occasion.

'C-can I speak to Mr Varley, please?' asked Keely, coming away from her thoughts.

'Mr Varley is rather busy today,' she was politely put off. 'Can I help in any way?'

Now she had got this far, anxiety was added to that awful despondency inside that she was being put off. She just could not face another uphill battle to find the courage to ring him a second time. 'It's Keely

Macfarlane here,' she said—then found that her anxiety was not needed, for just the mention of her name, it appeared, had a magical effect of getting her past Tarrant's watchdog.

'Just one moment, please, Miss Macfarlane,' said the secretary, her voice more forthcoming, 'I'll interrupt Mr Varley.'

Keely had time then only to hope that perhaps once she had told Tarrant about her miscarriage maybe she would start to feel less dejected. For in no time she was hearing his voice, and as weakness invaded her just to hear him, tears coming to her eyes, she was fighting desperately to find some stiffening from somewhere, as without introduction, he exploded:

'Keely! Where are you? Where in God's name have you been?'

She tried for a tart note, knowing full well that her old spirit would not have stayed down on being bellowed at, but it did not come off. Her voice was nowhere near as sharp as she would like to have heard it, as dully, she told him:

'It's no business of yours where I've been. Anyway, I'm back now, and I'm ringing you to . . .'

'Like hell it's no business of mine!' he cut her off. 'In case you've forgotten—you happen to be carrying my child!'

Oh, Tarrant, Keely wanted to sob as tears which wouldn't be denied at what he had just said welled to her eyes and rolled down her cheeks. But the moment had arrived to tell him, even if those words had to be pushed out to be heard.

'Not . . .' she began, and had to swallow more tears before she could continue. 'Not,' she said, her voice flat, without expression, 'any longer—I'm not.'

Tarrant's sharp intake of breath, followed by a clipped, 'What did you say?' just as if he couldn't believe his hearing, forced her to go on, to say those words that bit cruelly into her so that he should believe his hearing.

'I'm—no longer pregnant.'

The words had left her with pain. But it was like a stab to the heart when after a deathly silence while she tried to get more courage to tell him how she had inherited the family failing, a roar like that of a wounded tiger deafened her ears. Then she was being made to realise that her news, contrary to her expectation, had sent Tarrant into an inferno of rage such as the one she had seen on him before, as he went on to shatter her completely, the white heat of his fury scorching her ear drums as he snarled:

'You *bitch*! You cheating bloody bitch!'

'Cheating!' she echoed, never more taken aback, her voice no more than a whisper. 'I . . .'

But Tarrant was as mad as hell, she heard, and in no mind to let her in, as he went slamming into her with a vengeance. 'My God, it's no wonder I couldn't find you! I wasn't looking in the right places, was I? I should have started my search in specialised clinics, shouldn't I? To think I trusted your word! By God, will I know better than to . . .'

Unable to take any more, stunned that Tarrant was reviling her, shocked that he could think what he obviously was thinking, Keely quietly put down the phone.

Half an hour later, she was still in shock. She felt winded and down for the count. To have realised how much she had wanted his child, she was at rock bottom to know that when once he had accepted as her promise that she would not attempt to get rid of her precious cargo, Tarrant, without stopping to ask questions, had immediately believed the very worst of her.

Never having thought such an interpretation would be put on her absence, Keely was reeling from the knowledge that the man she had given her heart to had instantly drawn the conclusion that she had been hiding away in some clinic—having an abortion!

CHAPTER NINE

THAT Tarrant could believe what he had of her was on Keely's mind throughout the remainder of that Thursday. So much for hoping that to have told him would see an end to how depressed she felt! If anything, she felt worse than ever. Never had she known such hurt that he had jumped to the conclusion he had—nor would she ever forgive him.

It was no help with her desolation to have fairness give her a prod to ask what else he should have thought. She had taken herself off nearly two weeks ago without telling a soul where she was going, and the next he had heard from her was, without her dressing it up, her telling him that she was no longer pregnant.

He had called her a cheating bitch—not, she knew, because he had wanted that baby as much as she did, but because, a man of his word, he was furious that he thought she had broken her word to him.

Deeply hurt, her thoughts chasing one after the other only to come back to the same place, at just after nine that evening, Keely knew that she could not take this loneliness of spirit any longer. For going on two weeks now she had been alone with her sad thoughts and feelings, and, she owned, she desperately needed contact with someone who knew her well enough to know that whatever else she was—given Tarrant had deserved to be set up that time—she was not a cheat.

It was time she rang her mother anyway, she thought. Catherine would be expecting to hear from her until Saturday at the earliest.

Having bravely kept back tears since she had mopped herself up after her call to Tarrant, Keely was again to

148

feel the weakness of tears to hear Catherine, warmth in her voice, concern too, as she exclaimed:

'Keely! Oh, darling, where have you been? We've been worried to death about you!'

She had not wanted anyone to worry about her, but more guilt was heaped on her as she apologised and said, 'I had—a few things I wanted to work out.'

'You might have said,' her mother rebuked her gently. 'I had your message, of course, and Tarrant rang Gerald Cullen who said you'd taken two weeks of your holiday, but . . .' she broke off. 'Are you all right, Keely?' she asked sharply. 'You're not sounding like you at all.'

'I'm fine,' Keely replied, only to find that she had no chance of fooling per parent.

'You don't sound it,' answered Catherine, her voice concerned. She paused momentarily, and then said carefully, 'I'm doing my best not to interfere Keely, but—but I can't help but know that something must be wrong between you and Tarrant.'

'I'm not going to marry him,' Keely answered, striving hard to make her voice light, that or have her mother more concerned than ever.

'That's why you went away—to think about your engagement to Tarrant?'

Never having considered herself engaged to him in the first place, Keely found she could not lie to her mother about her reason for so hurriedly departing. But as she still could not speak, Catherine was drawing her own conclusions as, into the pause, she said:

'It's obviously your decision, not Tarrant's, to break your engagement.' But still Keely could find nothing to say. 'Does he know?' Catherine went on to question, revealing, 'The last time we saw him, he was still of the opinion that you were going to marry him.'

'He—knows now that we aren't going to be married,' said Keely, knowing that far from Tarrant wanting to marry her, she would be lucky if he ever so much as spoke to her again.

Another pause was to follow while Catherine digested what her daughter had said. Then she was stating, 'I'll accept that you haven't told Tarrant what you have without first thinking about it very deeply.' And, her love for her offspring showing through, she added gently, 'But you haven't come to that decision without it making you very unhappy, have you, darling?'

'I'm all right,' Keely insisted, feeling lower than ever that in effect she was lying to her mother by not telling her the truth. That when they had had few secrets between them, the secret she now held was one which she had to keep to herself.

'I know you better than that,' Catherine replied, and went on urgently, 'Come down to Inchbrook—you could stay for the weekend. You could . . .'

'I can't,' said Keely, butting in, though having to explain lest her mother should be hurt at her blunt refusal. 'I—don't want to—risk bumping into Tarrant.'

'I see.' Catherine thought for a moment, then with some of the same impulsiveness her daughter had inherited, 'I'll come up to see you, then. If I catch an early train tomorrow I can . . .'

'No, I don't want you to do that,' said Keely. In her view Lucas and Catherine had earned their enjoyment of each other's company. It wasn't right that through her they should spend so much as one day apart.

'But I don't like to hear you sounding so—so unlike you.'

Regretting that her mother had seen through her attempt to appear lighthearted, she was again protesting, 'I'm all right. Honestly I am,' though without success, for Catherine's tones sounded soothing as she came back:

'I'm sure you are.' Keely wondered if it might have been wiser to have left her phone call until Saturday, when surely another couple of days would see her losing

this constantly heavyhearted feeling, when Catherine
said suddenly, 'Can you hang on a moment.'

Guessing that she had just remembered she had a
cake to take out of the oven or something of that sort,
Keely held on, and in a very few minutes heard her
mother's voice again, different this time, and sounding
a shade happier.

'You're to come down first thing tomorrow,' she said
firmly. And before Keely could repeat her objection to
that, 'I've just spoken with Lucas,' she was informed,
'and he's positive that when he phones Tarrant and tells
him how you feel embarrassed at meeting him again
after breaking your engagement, Tarrant will do the
honourable thing and keep away from Inchbrook this
weekend.'

Keely went to bed that night with her every objection
overruled. But, lying sleepless, she could not help but
own to feeling relieved that tomorrow she was going to
Inchbrook. Even though she did not like to think that
she was keeping Tarrant out of his home, after having
had nearly two weeks of dragging around an
immovable heaviness of heart, surely, like before, just
the fact of having to show a cheerful face would see her
rising from that dark depression which she seemed
unable to get clear of?

Certain in her own mind that Tarrant would not care
a damn whether his presence at Inchbrook embarrassed
her or not, Keely got into the train on Friday morning
aware that, loathing her as he must, that was a more
accurate reason why Inchbrook would not see him until
she had left.

Without a smile in her, she determined as the train
rattled along that the moment she saw her mother and
Lucas, she was going to pin the brightest of smiles on
her face.

To see that both Catherine and Lucas were waiting
for her when she came out of the railway station was a
surprise she wasn't ready for. But though her smile was

a slow starter, she managed to curve her mouth upwards, only to have to choke back tears when her mother looked past her surface smile and into her sad eyes, and hugged her to her.

'Your room is all ready for you,' said Catherine cheerfully as she let go of her.

Shepherded to the Daimler, Keely took a seat in the back while her mother sitting beside Lucas in the front chattered on as he pulled away.

'We're having your favourite for lunch,' she said over her shoulder.

'And we thought we'd show you our favourite picnic spot this afternoon,' chipped in Lucas, to show her he bore her no ill will.

Keely guessed he had already been in touch with his son. Yet however angry Tarrant had been with her, she somehow knew that it was not his way to make things blacker for her with his father for having supposedly jilted him, by passing on to him just why, in effect, Tarrant had come to 'jilt' her.

Lunch was a satisfying meal, with Keely doing her best to consume a quantity of the meal her mother had prepared specially for her. But if her mother, who knew her so well, was aware of the effort involved for her to smile when the occasion demanded it, and to chatter back at the surface conversation Lucas started, then Keely was grateful to her that apart from a steady look at her now and then, Catherine made no mention of it.

The picnic spot turned out to be a meadow with a stream rippling near-by. And Keely could not help but feel a warmth that Lucas and Catherine had let her into the secret of their favourite place.

Though sadness flooded her again when the two of them went off to investigate a tree which should have finished blossoming by now but which, for some reason, was still splendid with blooms.

Lying on her back, the car rug spread on the ground

beneath her, Keely closed her eyes, thinking, as the sun beat down on her face, of the warmth in her mother, that openness in her parent that gave her the freedom to talk to her about simply anything.

A tear squeezed out between her lashes as she wished that she had told Catherine about her pregnancy. Oh, if only she had! Her mother had a wealth of experience about such matters; she would have been able to tell her the pitfalls to watch out for. She could have told her right from the very beginning what she, another victim of the Butterworth Factor, should and should not do. She might, she thought, as another tear strayed, had she been wise enough to seek her mother's advice, still carry that baby within her. Another tear strayed, its wetness as it rolled into her hairline making Keely pull herself up with a start.

She sat up, and looking over to where Lucas and Catherine had their backs to her, quickly brushed away the tears. By the time they had wandered back to her, she was dry-eyed and smiling.

But her hope that having to appear bright and cheerful might lift her leaden spirits was doomed to failure. For it was after dinner that night, as the three of them sat in the drawing room, that the dark cloud of depression she despaired of ever getting out from under came to totally encompass her.

Not wanting her mother or Lucas to recognise how down she was, Keely found the excuse she was looking for to go to her room when Lucas, referring to their picnic, remarked how the fresh air had done them all good.

'That fresh air is far more potent than I thought,' she replied. 'I think I'll have an early night.'

'You haven't been in bed by nine-thirty since before you were a teenager,' said Catherine, her gaze keen on her daughter's eyes.

From somewhere Keely's mouth found a grin. 'Guess I must be feeling my years,' she attempted to joke.

'Besides, I start work again on Monday—have to build up my strength for the fray.'

'You find Gerald Cullen a good man to . . .' Lucas's question halted in mid-air as the sound of a car coming up the drive was heard. 'That's . . .' he broke off, his eyes shooting to Catherine and then to Keely, his friendly smile fading, the sentence he had started needing no finishing to either of his listeners.

Oh God, Keely thought, her ears not so familiar as her stepfather's with the sound of different car engines, but her instinct knowing that had Lucas finished what he had started, he would have said, 'That's Tarrant's car!'

Her heart starting to thud painfully, she was unaware that two other people had gone as frozen as she. For as Lucas and Catherine just sat and looked at each other helplessly, and then at her, Keely felt too paralysed to move.

Even with her head telling her to get out of there, to go and get up to her room before Tarrant came and sought them, she found that she could not move, that her legs would not obey her.

Then it was too late to move. Footsteps were coming along the hall, and all too quickly, and before she had got herself anywhere near all of one piece, the door to the drawing room was opening. And as tall and as arrogant as ever, there stood Tarrant, his glance raking over all three of them.

His glance rested on her. And aggression and hatred were showing in those hard grey eyes the moment before he switched his look back to his father. Then he came further into the room to greet him.

By that time Lucas was halfway out of his chair, his voice severe as he collected himself, and said, 'I thought we'd agreed that you weren't coming home this weekend.'

'I don't recall any such agreement, sir,' Tarrant answered him respectfully, his eyes going over his father's shoulder to stare belligerently at Keely. 'My memory of our conversation is that you were of the opinion that my being in the company of Miss Macfarlane again might make her feel uncomfortable. I,' he went on, bringing his glance back to his father, 'merely agreed that it probably would.' With that Tarrant stepped past his father. 'Good evening, Catherine,' he greeted her politely. Then he turned to Keely.

And Keely needed only to see the ice that had hardened in his eyes as he looked coldly at her to know that, whether their respective parents were there or not, there was not the smallest likelihood that she would be on the receiving end of the same politeness he had extended to her mother.

She was not mistaken. For it was abruptly, doing away with any form of greeting and taking no account of her pale face, his very stance aggressive, that he asked bluntly:

'Does my presence make you feel uncomfortable?'

It was an effort to make herself look into those hard grey eyes. But where once she would have fired up at him, met his challenging remark head on, there was no fire in her when, for Catherine and Lucas's sake she made herself reply.

'No, not at all,' she said quietly.

She saw his eyes narrow at her passive answer. But when she saw a muscle jerk in his jaw, she knew then that at any moment that aggression in him that was barely hidden was going to come roaring to the surface. Again she was to find her surmise accurate.

'Then it damn well should!' he bit out angrily. 'After what you did, uncomfortable doesn't begin to cover what you should feel to face me!'

Having felt dead inside, anxiety started to flutter in her that in front of the other two Tarrant was going to reveal everything. But with no idea of how to stop him, only the knowing that she must—for Lucas would hit the roof if he told him now, and Tarrant had earned enough black marks from his father recently—Keely's anxious look turned from son to father.

But Lucas, obviously thinking that Tarrant was referring to the way she was supposed to have jilted him, was stepping in, his voice sharp as he remonstrated:

'Do you have to try and make Keely feel worse than she does already?'

'*She's* feeling rough!' Tarrant exploded, his angry look going from her to his father. 'How the hell do you think I'm feeling?'

Oh God, Keely thought, seeing that Lucas was beginning to look angry too at his son's tone. She knew without doubt that a full-scale row was going to break out at any moment—and she just couldn't take that.

'Please,' she begged, getting to her feet, taking a few paces forward to insert herself between them. 'Please— don't argue. I—don't—want that.'

'*You* don't want!' thundered Tarrant hostilely. She knew then that she had not helped matters, when, his tone sarcastic, cynically he apologised, 'Forgive me, Miss Macfarlane. I should have known without you having to tell me what it is you don't want. My only excuse is that I've only recently been made acquainted with how easy it is for you to break promises. Only just discovered how easy it is for you to discard what you *don't want.*'

'Tarrant!' she heard Lucas exclaim painfully. 'I know you've been hurt, son, but surely . . .'

Hurt! Keely turned away, not wanting to hear any more. 'I'm going to bed,' she told Catherine quietly, and knew that she didn't have the sole option on tears as the shine in her mother's eyes told her how upsetting she had found the scene, but because her daughter had been guilty of breaking her promise to marry Tarrant, there was not a thing she could say to intervene in her defence.

'Goodnight, love,' said Catherine gently.

Keely said goodnight to Lucas, but since Tarrant had his back to her and was helping himself from the whisky decanter, she was saved from so much as having to nod in his direction.

Feeling too dead inside for tears, she climbed despairingly into bed. Lucas had thought that the way Tarrant had gone for her stemmed from hurt. But she knew that it was nothing of the sort. The only thing wrong with Tarrant was that he was still furious with her in his belief that she had broken her word to him. And, deeply wounded, she knew she would never now tell him the truth.

That he had come home at all, when he knew full well that she would be there, was all the proof she needed to know that his fury with her had never waned. But that he still hated her, that that hate must be uppermost so that knowing where she would be that weekend, he had decided to be there too to have a go at her at every chance, was more than she could take.

Saddened in mind and spirit, Keely got out of bed the next morning knowing that her visit to Inchbrook was over. If Tarrant was staying for the rest of the weekend ready to unleash his anger with her at the smallest opportunity, then any hope of her putting a bright face on it had gone.

Not that she wanted to make a fuss about leaving. It was, after all, Tarrant's home, and she didn't want his father angry with him again if he thought his son was driving her out.

Deciding to have a quiet word with her mother, but unsure, remembering that Tarrant was no stranger to the kitchen before breakfast, that she would find her mother alone there, she thought she would wait to have that quiet word until she was helping her clear up in the kitchen after breakfast. Sure that Catherine would see it would be better all round that she went, Keely stayed in her room until she thought breakfast would be on the table. Only then did she leave her room to go downstairs.

Not feeling hungry, she had no wish for anyone to think she was avoiding Tarrant. Though not wanting a private confrontation with him, she was sure, as she turned the handle of the breakfast room door, that she had left it late enough for everyone to be assembled.

To find that the only other person in the breakfast room was Tarrant made her want to back out quickly. But as he turned from his silent contemplation of the garden and saw her, there was no chance of that.

'Don't hover, Miss Macfarlane,' he said loftily as he came away from the windows. 'Come in.'

Knowing that her decision to leave had been a right one, without saying a word, Keely moved to the seat she had used before when breakfasting at Inchbrook. With her eyes on her place setting, she was still able to observe that Tarrant had moved to take the chair exactly opposite her.

But oh, how she wished she could leave without having to wait for that quiet word with her mother. For Tarrant was starting the day as he meant to go on, and was dead set on baiting her, it seemed, as he asked, a pleasantness in his voice she had no belief in:

'You weren't sick this morning, I trust?'

Feeling a knife stab to her heart, she swallowed hard on the knot of pain his question had caused. Oh, how she would welcome that particular sign that she still carried his child!

'No,' she replied, her voice as dull and as lifeless as she felt.

But if she had hoped that her quiet answer would see Tarrant tiring of his baiting game before it had begun, then she was to be sorely disappointed when, determined it seemed to get some reaction from her, he went on to remark:

'What a strange effect guilt has on you, Miss Macfarlane.'

Slowly Keely raised her eyes to his cynical mocking face. 'Guilt?' she questioned, her eyes going wide as she wondered how he knew of the guilt that riddled her that she had been so mindless of that cherished gift that had been so briefly hers.

'Where's the passion I once knew?' he answered, going on to show that it was not the guilt of her carelessness he had seen or was referring to, but the guilt he thought she should feel to have done what he believed of her. 'It's not like you to be meek and mild, Miss Macfarlane. Has the heavy burden of the guilt you *should* feel taken the stuffing from you?' he enquired sarcastically. 'Has that overwhelming guilt sapped all the spirit in you?' he went on to mock.

'Please—Tarrant,' said Keely huskily. 'Please don't . . .'

'Please, Tarrant,' he threw back in her face roughly, that word 'don't' clearly getting to him. 'After what you did I feel perfectly at liberty to say and do to you whatever I please.' And, having not by any means finished with her yet, 'You don't feel an ounce of compunction over what you did, do you?' he charged. 'It didn't so much as dawn on you how I would feel to hear my father tell me that you and I were no longer engaged.'

'You knew that anyway,' she said quietly, but felt unable to cope with the fresh charge he was laying at her door, that of throwing him over and letting him be the last one to know. 'It was you who jilted me, not the other way around.'

'When did I do that?' he asked sharply.

But she wasn't in the mood for any more of his baiting. 'Does it matter?' she asked, lowering her eyes, that dark ceiling of depression coming down over her. 'There seems little point in discussing it, since there's no reason now for you to marry me.'

'You thought you'd made bloody sure of that, didn't you?' he snarled back before she could blink.

And, looking for an outlet for his aggression when she made no answer, he found that outlet as he fairly roared at her, words raining thick and furious about her bent head, something, as tears started to well up in her, which she didn't need just then.

'Without so much as waiting to hear my plans—not bothering to wait for me to call that evening so we could discuss everything, *you* decided what *you alone* wanted, and had booked yourself into a clinic before I'd so much as completed my first day back at my desk!'

Keely held hard on to her tears. But when not a peep came from her in her defence, her very silence appeared to serve only to infuriate him more.

'My stars!' ripped from him when she would not so much as look at him. 'God knows what it is you *are* feeling, that you're sitting there without firing back at me in your usual manner—but it certainly isn't guilt!'

Struggling for words, slowly Keely raised her unhappy face, the tears only just in check. 'I . . .' she began, and faltered, sorely in need of the spirit which Tarrant had recognised was missing in her. But that numbed feeling inside was too solid for spirit of any kind to find a foothold. 'I . . . I'll go—and see if I can help my mother,' she told him quietly, desperately wanting to be away from him.

Aware that Tarrant was wearing a disbelieving look to see that the full-spirited girl who had once served his face a vicious swipe by way of introduction had suddenly turned into a girl who was backing away from a fight, Keely went to leave the table. But before she could more than move her chair back, he was staying her, his anger seeming to have left him, his expression appearing more puzzled by her than angry, as he said:

'By the sound of it, Catherine has done everything there is to be done.'

Keely, not as familiar as he with the different sounds in the house, had not heard the kitchen door closing.

But in a very few seconds her mother was joining them, her glance going from one to the other. And since she had not heard Tarrant positively roaring at her daughter a minute before, her greeting to them both was easy, her look revealing to Keely that she was hopeful that they had got any embarrassment out of the way, and that things could now progress more favourably than they had begun last night.

'Belatedly,' said Keely, as Tarrant stood up to pull out Catherine's chair, 'I was just coming to help you.'

'No need,' said Catherine, her manner easy still. 'Lucas insisted on wheeling the trolley in, only he got waylaid by the postman at the door.' She turned her attention from her daughter, her smile going to the door as just then Lucas, pushing the trolley before him, followed in its wake.

Her heart not in it, Keely did her best to join in the surface conversation that followed as Catherine served out bacon and eggs and Lucas doled out the mail, she being the only one without an envelope addressed to her.

'There's a batch of circulars here you can have,' Lucas teased, when each had a couple of letters apiece, and making her feel part of the foursome family, her mother led the way by opening her correspondence as was the habit in the Varley household at the breakfast table.

Keely smiled back at him as she shook her head. 'I've probably had duplicates of those delivered to my flat this morning.'

'One from Aunt Shelagh,' Catherine addressed her, having slit both her envelopes and deciding she wanted to read the communication from her sister first. 'I'll let you have a read of it in a minute.'

Keely cut into bacon she did not want, Tarrant within her range of vision not having anything to say as he took up his correspondence.

That was until the sudden distressed cry of, 'Oh no!'

left her mother's lips. Then he was there to ask with Lucas:

'Something wrong, Catherine?'

Her mother read on for a few more seconds, then as Keely asked, 'Has something happened to Aunt Shelagh?' she lowered her letter to look sadly at her.

'Not Shelagh,' she said gravely. 'It's Jeanette.'

'What . . .' was as far as Keely got, before Catherine was saying:

'Oh, the poor dear child! She's lost her baby.'

'Oh *no*!' cried Keely, entirely unaware that Tarrant's eyes had left her mother and were on her at the wealth of distress in her exclamation. But, mindless of him just then, all Keely could think of was her poor poor cousin Jeanette who, further along with her pregnancy than she had been, had so wanted her baby. Oh, how very dreadful Jeanette must be feeling!

'It's awful news, isn't it?' agreed Catherine. 'I must write to the child by return. If she's feeling anywhere at all as low as I, and her mother too, used to feel when we miscarried, then she must be in a dreadful state of depression.' As if suddenly aware then that the two men present, not knowing her niece, would find little interest in what she was saying, Catherine's eyes left Keely's and went to smile at Lucas, as, her voice tailing off, she murmured, 'It used to knock the spirit right out of me whenever I suffered a miscarriage.'

Keely was glad that her mother had ended that particular conversation. It did her own feeling of depression no good to hear that her poor cousin had fallen victim to that part of the Butterworth Factor too.

But it was while she was thinking that once she was back in her flat, she too would write to commiserate with Jeanette, that Keely was suddenly aware that where Lucas, after a sympathetic word, had patted her mother's hand and had taken up his knife and fork and that her mother was reading through her sister's letter again, there was a strange sort of tension coming from Tarrant's direction.

Her eyes lowered, she saw from the correspondence that lay by his plate that he was taking no further interest in his mail. Her eyes then went to his hands which were making no attempt to take up his eating implements. Then it was that she saw that his knuckles were showing—white! Slowly her eyes went from his hands—and up to his face.

To find that his eyes were fixed on her and at nothing or no one else, made her green eyes widen. But as she stared dumbly at him, so she was to see that if he did not have one single smile to spare for her, then neither was there any of the aggression there which she had expected to see whenever those grey eyes found hers!

She was to see then that alertness in his look she had seen before. That particular look that had been there when his mind had been investigating and searching for some truth. And Keely knew, as she saw his hands go seemingly casually out of sight beneath the table and he turned his attention from her and on to her mother, that his brain was going ten to the dozen.

'Do I gather from what you've just said, Catherine,' she heard him ask, 'that you frequently miscarried in pregnancy?'

'I'm sorry,' her mother replied, while Keely was getting on to Tarrant's wavelength, and wishing she wasn't, 'it isn't quite a subject for the breakfast table, is it—It was just that I was so shocked to hear that my poor niece Jeanette has inherited every aspect of what we in the family call the Butterworth Factor.'

'The Butterworth Factor?' he questioned, and for the first time in her life Keely wished her mother would shut up and not say anything more.

But Catherine had caught that, breakfast table or no, Tarrant appeared genuinely interested. And maybe because yesterday Lucas had gone out of his way to show her daughter that he bore her no ill will, she was going on to answer Tarrant, to show that she too felt the same about her husband's son.

'It dates from way back,' she told him. 'Butterworth being the name of one of my forebears. Hence the name "Butterworth Factor" which all the females in the line risk when they decide to start a family.'

'The risk being,' Tarrant took up, his mind, Keely felt, having gone to work overtime, 'that whomsoever the Butterworth Factor visits stands a very real chance of miscarrying?'

Catherine nodded, and seeing from the way Lucas was tucking into his bacon and eggs that nothing was going to put him off his breakfast, she expanded, 'It's an ever-present hazard.' And with Tarrant showing such keen interest, she appeared to have forgotten that he had once been going to be her daughter's husband, and went on to confide, 'but one which I hope Keely will escape when her time comes, because it doesn't seem at all fair, when one considers the terrible time the Butterworth women willingly go through, that that whole dreadful time should end in grief accompanied by such a fearful feeling of dejection, against one's will.'

As Catherine finished speaking and she went to pour Lucas a cup of coffee, so Tarrant's eyes shot to Keely. But as unsmiling as he, Keely looked back, when she saw he had lost some of his colour, she knew that what she had last night thought never to tell him was known to him by some other means.

She knew it for a fact before, his voice strained, he said hoarsely, 'Keely,' oblivious that both Catherine and Lucas had looked up sharply to hear that sound in his tone. 'My dear . . .' he said, but his voice was thick in his throat and he seemed quite unable to go on.

Had Keely been able to hold back her tears while his roaring aggression had been battering her, then that softer, gentler note was her undoing. Tears flooded to her eyes, tears she could not have stopped no matter how hard she tried. Tears that her mother, Lucas, but worst of all Tarrant, could not fail to see.

She saw his hands come from under the table. Those same hands stretching out to her over the white table-cloth as if by no known impulse in him, but as if it was instinctive in him to touch, to comfort.

'Why—couldn't you tell me?' he asked throatily. 'Why didn't you?'

And Keely could not take it. Her eyes blinded by tears, she did not see her mother swallow, nor did she see that Lucas was looking amazed at this gentleness from his son for the girl who last night he had lost no time in pitching into.

All Keely caught was a glimpse through shimmering tears of Tarrant and the hands she ignored. With tears streaming down her cheeks she left the table and raced from the room before anyone had had time to recover from their individual cases of shock.

CHAPTER TEN

KEELY'S first action on reaching her room was to take out her case and begin filling it. That Tarrant knew now that he had accused her unjustly, that he was totally shocked on learning the truth, was something she could not help him with.

She wanted to get away, and now. She did not want to wait around for any apology from him, if apology it was to be. For, knowing Tarrant as she did, he would be quickly over his shock, and any apology he had to make would be mixed in with fresh accusation. It had already been there in part before she had bolted from the breakfast room, hadn't it? There in that question of 'Why couldn't you tell me?'

Closing her case, Keely lifted it from the bed and went quickly to her bedroom door. She felt used up and incapable of going into explanations. What her mother or Lucas thought, she didn't know. Though Tarrant being Tarrant, she wouldn't put it past him to have told them all that there was to know. And, feeling as she did, if it was to be sympathy from her mother, or a scene if there had been a row downstairs, she just hadn't got any reserves left to face it.

But if she had been hoping to leave Inchbrook without meeting anyone on her way out, then as she opened her bedroom door and saw a grim-faced Tarrant standing there, her hopes were split asunder.

Whether he had just arrived or whether he had been waiting outside her door for her to appear, Keely had no way of knowing. But after her initial start of surprise when instinct would have made her smartly close the door again, with control she thought she no longer had, she managed to ignore that impulse. Just as she meant to ignore Tarrant as, her glance sliding from his taut expression, she went to go past him.

A firm hand coming to her arm stopped her. That firm hand turned her about as, without a word leaving him, Tarrant pushed her back into her room and closed the door after them.

Resignation set in then when, his aim achieved, he let go her arm and allowed her to walk a few paces away. She had nothing she wanted to say to him, but since he obviously had something he wanted to say to her, she hoped he would soon say it and leave her to get on with her intention to go back to London.

She went over to the window, leaving Tarrant to address her back as she stared listlessly out, his voice having a tight control to it as, with no sign of apology, he asked:

'Why didn't you tell me you'd miscarried our child?'

So it was to be accusation! Not caring very much any more, she gave a defeated shrug of her shoulders. 'You didn't give me the chance,' she replied tonelessly—only to find that he was still accusing:

'*You* hung up on *me*,' he reminded her.

'I was expected to stay talking to you after what you'd said?' she asked, but there was no heat in her voice. Though having got started, it became easier for her to talk. 'As I remember it,' she found herself going on, 'after I'd told you about . . .' her voice broke. But hearing a sound that told her that Tarrant had moved and must be standing somewhere very close behind, she caught at sufficient control to continue, 'You were far too busy believing I was a cheating bitch to want to hear anything else anyway.'

A hand touched her shoulder as Tarrant attempted to turn her to face him, and it did nothing for her efforts to keep hold of the small self-control she had just mustered. She tugged away from him and went to stand at the foot of the bed, her brow puckering that he was making no attempt to defend the fact that it had been the blunt way she had told him he was no longer to be a father, that had set him off.

He was making no excuses for himself, and her love for him was such that, although only two days ago she had thought she would never forgive him for what he had said and thought, she was soon making excuses for him. She went on:

'But then you wouldn't have believed me. From the very first you've taken delight in disbelieving everything you could of me.'

That was true too, she thought, wishing she could feel angry, wishing she could find that spark that would make her feel more alive than she had been feeling just recently.

Tarrant coming to put a hand on each of her shoulders told her she was not as dead inside as she had thought. Told her that she wanted to feel alive. She didn't want to feel this way, when just his touch could fracture her vulnerability.

'Don't—do that,' she said, an urgency in her that hadn't been there before as the thumb of his right hand stroked in small movements over her collarbone. 'Emotionally, I don't know where I am.' Immediately she wanted those words back, and hurriedly she explained so that he should know that it was not his touch that had sent her emotions haywire, 'You accused me of feeling guilty, and I do. So much so that my emotions are all over the place.'

'So tell me about it, Keely,' Tarrant said quietly behind her. 'Tell me about these all-over-the-place emotions in you. I—want to help.'

Her eyes fastened on her case where he had set it down over by the door, and she shook her head in refusal to tell him anything of how she was feeling. 'It's far better if I go now,' she told him, and moved forward, owning some small surprise that he let her go, making no physical attempt to keep her there.

But when he said, 'If I haven't been fair to you in the

past Keely, then I don't think you are being very fair to me now,' she was to halt before she reached the door.

The feel of his touch with her still, she half turned. She looked at him fully then, seeing him as tall and straight—Tarrant with his 'own up and take the consequences' philosophy; Tarrant, her lover of one night and with whom, for her, there could be no future.

'I don't understand,' she stayed to reply, something in her urging her to go, but that compelling quality he had for her keeping her feet rooted.

'I know I've forfeited any right to expect the fairness I denied you,' he replied. 'But since, ultimately, I'm the cause of you being out of gear emotionally, don't you think it's only right that I should have the chance to try and help now, when before, I was of no help at all?'

That word 'ultimately' struck her with fear that he had guessed at the love she bore him. And desperately then she was trying to get herself together, needing as she did to be ready when the time came to deny such a charge as totally ridiculous. Though she had to swallow hard before she could find her voice to ask:

'What do you mean—that you're the ultimate cause?'

'The Butterworth Factor,' he replied to confuse her, going on to show that he had not missed one tiny word of what her mother had revealed to him. 'Had it not been for me, Keely, you wouldn't now be suffering from the lowness of spirit that's taken you. Can't you see that I want to help you with this depression that has you in its grip if I can?' An encouraging smile, which was to do nothing for her faint strength, left him. 'Can't you see that I need to help?' he asked.

Her legs feeling suddenly weak from relief that he had not seen her love for him, as much as from the havoc his encouraging smile had wrought, Keely, sorely needing to sit down, found that she had at some stage moved farther into the room and was standing at the opposite side of the bed from him. Without her being quite aware of her action, instinct took her to sit at the

end of the bed as her mind tried to see what it was that
Tarrant was telling her.

'I'd—forgotten that the child would have been
yours too,' she said, and had to wonder at that
statement, since it was more that she had lost
something precious which he had given her that was
in a large degree responsible for the way she was
feeling. Thoroughly confused, she added, 'Perhaps
that's why . . .'

She broke off abruptly, knowing she had very nearly
given herself away. Then she knew more confusion as,
moving quietly, Tarrant came to sit on the bed beside
her.

Clearing her throat, she began again. 'I'm sorry, I'm
not making much sense, am I?'

'You're doing fine,' he encouraged, with such an
abundance of kindness that tears she was determined
not to shed stung the backs of her eyes. 'Let's sort out
this guilt thing that's bugging you for a start, shall we?'
he suggested, still in that same kind way.

Keely did not know where to start. She was not even
sure she wanted to tell him anything about it. But his
suggestion that she wasn't being very fair to him, that
he needed to share, needed to help if he could, made her
see that maybe prospective fathers needed to wash
away guilt too.

'I wouldn't—have—deliberately given that life up,'
she started slowly. And, getting her bearings, she found
speech becoming easier again. 'No matter what battles
have gone on, or would have gone on between you and
me, I wouldn't have done that.'

'Perhaps one of these days you'll find it in you to
forgive me for ever daring to think such a thing,'
murmured Tarrant by her side. But clearly he was not
expecting her to forgive him for some time, for gently
he was urging, 'Go on, Keely.'

She hesitated, having lost track for a moment. Then,
painfully, she was confessing, 'I feel so guilty that in my

inexperience, yet when I knew all about the Butterworth Factor . . .' Suddenly it was all coming out in a rush. 'When I'd heard enough about it to know that the smallest thing can trigger it off, that—when Gerald took me home from work that day you phoned, I should start to feel so much better that . . .' she had to break off to hold back more tears, 'that like I had several times before, I decided t-to change my furniture around. It never dawned on me until . . .'

Helplessly she had to break off again—and was near to breaking down when in a gesture of sympathy, of understanding, Tarrant's arm came around her shoulders.

'When did it happen?' he asked, set, she realised, on getting it all out of her system.

'That night,' she replied, her voice going choky. And quickly then she was imploring him, 'Don't be kind to me,' and having to excuse, 'For the life of me I can't seem to find any stiffening.' And striving with all she had to summon up a smile, 'I think you'd better go, Tarrant. I—I think there's a very g-good chance that I'm in for another howling session.'

'Poor little love,' he soothed gently, which as a help in getting herself together, had a negative result. 'Never am I going to be unkind to you again.'

'Promises!' she managed to retort, but knew that she was fighting a losing battle with her tears. 'Please go,' she pleaded urgently.

But Tarrant shook his head. 'I should have been with you on those other occasions when you howled your eyes out,' he said quietly. And then effectively he gave her something else to think about, when he added quietly, his grey eyes fixed on hers. 'Besides which, this is one of the few times I've had a conversation with you when you're not laying into me—this may be my one and only chance to get to you.'

'Get to me?' she questioned, confused again.

'Call me what you will, it certainly isn't gentlemanly

to take advantage of the situation. But in this instance, the stakes are too high for that to worry me.'

Her bewilderment showed, as again she had to own, 'I don't under . . .'

'Normally sweet Keely,' he said, causing her heartbeats to go erratic, her need to have a good howl getting left behind somewhere, 'you're so spirited in your opposition that I have to resort to telling you what I want rather than ask and wait politely for your answer.'

'You have something you want to ask me?' she questioned, doing her best to keep up with him. 'Something which you think—if you ask now—I—might agree to without putting up any opposition?'

'I know I must be crass to expect to hear the answer I dearly want to hear,' he replied softly. 'But I'm hoping I can persuade you to—my point of view.'

'Without a fight, do you mean?' she asked, puzzling it out as she went along. 'Because you've seen that I don't appear to have any—fight in me any more—you think I'll hear what you have to say first?'

'The fight in you will come back,' Tarrant promised solemnly. 'But before it does—and before you start slamming into me in no uncertain terms for daring to think what I did of you—will you give me your promise to partner me in making use of the special licence that's been burning a hole in my pocket ever since the day I collected it?'

'Spe . . .' Open-mouthed, Keely was understanding no better now than when she had tried to see what it was he had to ask her.

'Will you marry me?' Tarrant asked earnestly. 'I can soon arrange it. Just say . . .'

'Marry you!'

Suddenly, having thought she was near to being dead inside, as pink colour washed her face, so life was stirring in her. Shock was pushing her out of that depression she had despaired of ever being free from.

Shock and hope. Though hope was to begin to fade, even as Tarrant took hold of her hands to say:

'Believe me, I have no wish to make you feel worse than you do right now. But please, Keely—please marry me.'

What conversation had been between them up until that moment went promptly from her mind. Only one certain fact presented itself to her, and no other. Somewhere along the line, Tarrant must have misunderstood. Though how could that be? Keely was suddenly too mixed up to hope to find the answer.

'But I'm—I'm not pregnant any longer,' she said. And she was sure then, as the fog in her head started to clear, that he was aware of that fact. 'You know that,' she added. 'You heard me . . .'

'I heard you,' he agreed. 'But my prop . . .' The shaking of her head cut him off.

Keely had no time then in which to go into the reasons why he was asking her to marry him. Time only to know that she had to stop this talk of their marrying before it went any further. To stop it before this weakness in her made her give in to anything he asked of her.

'I don't want to be married,' she followed up the shake of her head. And her words went racing one after the other in case she proved less strong than she had to be. 'I've already decided that my future lays in a career. I like business life. I enjoy my work. I . . .'

All encouragement faded from his face, and that toughness was back, as Tarrant cut her off, 'You intend to make your career with Cullen's firm—with Cullen?'

Crazily, the ridiculous idea that Tarrant sounded jealous at the thought of her continuing to work for Gerald occurred to Keely. She knew then that her confusion had a lot to answer for. Though with Tarrant bringing Gerald's name up, she had to pause to think— did she want to go on working for him?

'Maybe not with Gerald,' she answered honestly. 'I like him. Sometimes I'm even fond of him, but . . .'

'But you're not in love with him?' he asked, that sharp note she had idiotically mistaken for jealousy still there.

Again she shook her head. 'No, I'm not in love with him,' she replied, and as his expression lightened a little, she told him truthfully, 'I worry about Gerald's—regard—for me sometimes. I—don't think it would be fair to him to continue to work . . .'

'Do you think you're being fair to me? Do you think it's fair to refuse to marry me?' Tarrant asked sharply—and gave her no time to puzzle the answer to what he could be meaning, but enlightened her just the same as he went on, 'Your mother—my father—they both expect us to marry. And, I might say, are delighted for us.'

'But—they know that we're not going to . . .' she tried to protest.

'You think they aren't downstairs now putting two and two together?' he came in. 'Though they're both doing their best not to interfere, do you think you running out of the breakfast room the way you did, with me still grappling with shock coming after you, hasn't got them thinking that our engagement is far from being over?'

Keely had not had a chance to go into what her mother or Lucas would be thinking. But delighted though she had to agree both parents had been at the thought of the two of them going to marry, their delight was just not a good enough reason for her and Tarrant to take that step.

'They'll get over it,' she said, starting to feel lifeless again as she trotted out what she knew to be true. 'My mother, in any case, has very decided views on marriage. She wouldn't want me to marry when love is not there.'

A muscle tightened in Tarrant's jaw, but it was not

from any anger in him, she discovered. Though he was not letting up in his determination to get to her when her ability to fight him was at a low ebb.

'Love could come if you let it,' he told her, when Keely was desperate to keep from him that her love was already there, it was *his* love she was talking about, or rather, his lack of love for her. 'I know I've been a bastard to you,' he went on to press. 'But it isn't as if we have to get married, is it—which was your main objection the last time I asked you to marry me.'

As far as she could remember, there had not been very much asking about it. But as she began to realise that Tarrant did not seem to be going to give up easily, so she saw that she would just have to find some fight from somewhere to oppose him.

'Don't you see,' she asked, 'that with that objection out of the way, there simply isn't any reason for us to marry?'

But with Tarrant seeming to see some reason to hold back, yet still looking as if he still saw a reason for them to marry, Keely found her intelligence was stirring from its mass of confusion. And she found then that she was delving for answers, the way she had seen his mind go to work when he wanted answers.

'Is it because of the love and respect you have for your father that you want to marry me?' she found herself asking. 'Is it—that knowing he would be delighted,' she ploughed her way through, 'you—just—want to please him?'

'When I marry,' Tarrant answered without hesitation, 'it will be to please myself.'

Knowing, not surprisingly that she was on the wrong track, Keely felt something else stir inside her beside intelligence. Not that her intelligence had proved all that bright, she had to own. But pride was jolted into her, and with that pride, a touch of anger that had long since been absent, as a shade tartly, she asked:

'Then you want to marry me because you feel sorry

for me?' She saw from his alert look at her change of tone that he had recognised that the old Keely Macfarlane was coming to life, but she was angry still as she threw at him, 'You've at last realised that I'm nothing like the person you've believed me to be.'

'I'm sorry, yes,' he agreed, his eyes holding hers. 'Regretful, yes. Remorseful too, for every vile thing I've ever said to you. But,' he added, to send all anger flying from her, 'I want to marry you only because—because I want to.'

It was then as she looked away from him that she saw what she should have seen at the start. What Tarrant had seen when she had not wanted him to. He knew she was in love with him!

She made a move as if to get up and put some space between them, but Tarrant's arm came around her shoulders again, and tightened, and she felt too defeated by then to do battle. But she could no longer look at him, as a groan left her, and she said:

'Oh, Tarrant!' And when he quietly just held her like that, words were then leaving her, words which she had never thought she would say to him. 'You're a kind person, aren't you?'

Not looking at him, she had no idea how he reacted to hear her say that. But she was going on, seeing now that with Tarrant so remorseful for all the vile things he had said to her, having taken her, having seen her love for him, to marry her—was his way of trying to make amends.

'There's such a wealth of kindness in you,' she went on, her voice growing husky. 'I should have seen your reasoning before, only I didn't.'

The grip he had on her increased momentarily. And there was a gruff note in the voice that reached her ears, when he asked:

'You—know now why I want to marry you?'

'Oh yes,' she replied on a sigh, her eyes on her lap. 'There's a caring in you I forgot about, but which was there in the way you attempted to make my mother leave when you thought she was taking your father for a ride. That same caring was there when in the kitchen that Sunday you looked after me when I felt so dreadful. That same caring,' she went on, fighting her way through mists of what was suddenly becoming confused, 'that morning you rang Gerald, not—giving away why I was sick when I thought that in order to get your own way that was what you had done. Your caring...' Without warning she broke off, not sure when she had started to substitute the word 'caring' for 'kindness'.

Then hot colour was suffusing every inch of her, her heart starting to pound out a suffocating beat that left her breathless, so that although she knew her colour was high, she lifted her eyes to stare at Tarrant.

'I don't think, Kecly,' he said slowly, a tenseness in him, in the arm he still had around her, 'that you'd quite got to the reason why I find it imperative that you marry me. But,' he went on, a seriousness in his face that was as tense as the rest of him, as in the way that was his, he faced whatever consequences there were to be, 'keep going, I think you're almost there.'

Her breathing coming in gulps, Keely fastened on to what she knew so far, making herself go on because suddenly Tarrant's coming to her room after her, his insistence on staying, everything, seemed to have a different, more overwhelming significance. Hastily she backtracked to where that caring he had shown for his father had stemmed from the one and only fact that he respected and—loved him. And though she knew it was impossible, she had to let her thoughts push on the way they wanted to go. Did that then mean—when she just knew that it didn't—that—that Tarrant loved her just a little, that he—cared for her!

'Tarrant,' she said, wanting to know with a fever of urgency, but feeling too scared to ask, 'when—when you were c-caring—er—looking after me that Sunday, when you sent me back to bed and brought me tea, was it—me you were concerned about or, was it . . .'

'The baby,' he said, coming in to help her out, 'was a bond between us. A bond,' he added levelly, not taking his eyes from hers, 'which the more I thought about, the more I began to like. It became a bond I so badly needed to have that when that bond was broken, I couldn't take it without becalling you.'

Her heartbeats chaotic, knowing that there was every chance she was going to come to earth with a thud, Keely stared at him as though hypnotised.

'But,' he went on, 'while there can be other infants—and I'll see to it that you have all the specialised attention from the word go the next time—there can only be one you for me.'

Her mouth gone dry, her voice was only the merest thread of sound, as she dared to ask:

'You—care—a little, for me?'

Tarrant's free hand came to take hold of her hands in her lap, and he looked at her solemnly for long moments. Then with that hand gripping hers, honestly, he told her:

'If going slowly out of my mind when you did your disappearing act—if being constantly on the phone here in case you'd rung again—if forgetting about my work half the time to go searching for you, is caring a little—then God help me, Keely Macfarlane, should it be possible that I should care more?'

Trembling, she wanted to say, you mean, you love me, but her voice let her down before she could get further than:

'You . . .'

'I,' he told her, without her knowing it, receiving some encouragement from her gentle eyed wonderous look, 'have known myself drawn to you since that might in my flat when, sure I didn't give a damn where you slept, I found I was offering you my bed.'

'Y-you've been—drawn to me,' she whispered.

'And fighting it like hell,' he confessed. 'I was far too busy to come down to Inchbrook that weekend before I went to Australia, but when I knew that you'd be here, it was this way I found myself heading—only to be angry at recognising jealousy when I learned that Cullen was here too. And angry again that I should feel so inordinately pleased at my first sight of you in the garden.'

He was going too fast for her. There were so many questions that bubbled to the surface. But it was astonishment that made her ask only one of those many questions.

'You were—jealous—of Gerald?' she asked, her eyes widening.

'Your face beamed a smile that was meant for him until you turned—that smile soon disappeared when you saw it was me.'

'I was sure there was only hate between us then,' Keely murmured in defence—and saw that Tarrant looked pleased at that word 'then', although it was he who had gone to look a shade hesitant, as he asked:

'You're—feeling a little– differently about me now?'

Unsure of herself, having the wonderful knowledge that Tarrant did care a little for her, by the sound of it, more than a little, a mixture of emotions rioting in her, Keely found she could not tell him.

'I . . .' she began, but still wondering about the extent of his caring for her. If he had started to care right from that night she had spent in his flat after the wedding, if he had felt jealousy that weekend he had spent a night in her flat, then how far did that caring extend? If he cared for her so much, then how much caring was there in him for her that having driven them angrily to her flat, having made love to her, he could leave her with nothing more than a phone call when she got to the office, and the intimation that he did not want to see her again?

As he watched the emotions playing about her face,

Tarrant's voice had gone serious when he asked, 'What's wrong, Keely?' And it was sternly that he followed that up when, unable to answer him, she shook her head. 'I've been afraid to rush you,' he told her firmly, 'in case a wrong word had you feeling worse than you have been feeling. To prevent that I've hung back and let you see for yourself how things are with me. But,' he said, not letting go his hold on her, 'I think you must see by now that we've come too far to leave any skeletons hiding away in dark cupboards.'

He was right, she saw. They had come *too* far. Too much had gone on between them. If anything was to be resolved, either by some amicable agreement that would see them, if it couldn't be avoided, bumping into each other at Inchbrook for her mother and Lucas's sake, without animosity, or for her to discover that which she dared not yet believe in, then she had to be brave enough to bring all her skeletons out of the cupboard, and to take the risk of not liking the answers she received.

But it was a moment or two before she could get herself sufficiently together to bring herself to ask:

'That night—that night before you went to Australia.' From the change in his expression, the contrite look that came over him, Keely knew he was right there with her. 'That night you stayed in my flat,' she went on. 'Why did you leave when you awakened without waking me? Was it because you—hated me then?'

'Hated you!' He looked so taken aback that she just knew that whatever emotion had been in him then, it had not been hate. 'Good God!' he exclaimed, and looked staggered.

Though imagining she could think such a thing, or might still be thinking it, made him swiftly put his shock to one side as he went on quickly to tell her:

'I never so much as closed my eyes that night. Bitter compunction I'd never expected to feel kept me sleepless. You'll never know how I felt to have you

weeping in my arms. But as dawn started to break and I
saw innocence in your face, for all I'd taken your
innocence from you, I knew then that I couldn't stay
for you to wake up. I knew I couldn't stay to see the
loathing of me that would be in your eyes at what I'd
done. I discovered that I, who've never backed away
from anything in my life, just could not take that.'
Gently then, his confession of how it had been out in
the open, Tarrant told her, 'I couldn't even face
myself—so how could I face you when I'd just begun to
realise that it was not your loathing I wanted?'

'Oh,' said Keely softly, trying hard to collect herself.
'So your phone call to the office wasn't to tell me to
make use of your absence to get all my visits to
Inchbrook out of the way before you returned?'

'My God!' he replied, looking stupefied that she had
seen his phone call that way. And shaking his head as
though to clear it, sincerely he told her, 'I found I
couldn't leave the country without a word. But with
your hatred of me unmistakable on the phone, hatred
which I knew I deserved, that didn't stop me from
getting rattled. But it was in Australia that I realised
why I couldn't take your hating me. In Australia when
my hand went to the phone a dozen times to call you.
In Australia that I wrote to you to . . .'

'I didn't receive any letter from you!'

'I didn't post any,' Tarrant replied. 'But in that long
month I wrote to you many times, only to scrap each
one as I saw that, hating me as you must, there wasn't
anything I could write that would change that. It was
the longest month of my life,' he confessed. 'My first
thought when I eventually got back was to ring you.'

'But you didn't.'

'I rang my father instead. He told me that Catherine
had a cold, which since by then I was sorely needing to
see you,' he said to thrill her, 'had me thinking up a
way to get you down to Inchbrook for the weekend.'

'My mother's cold rapidly developed into 'flu,' said

Keely, a warm glow spreading through her, no thought in her to be angry with him.

'To my mind, nothing else would have you talking to me for longer than it took to slam the door shut on me,' he owned, going on, 'You can't begin to know the feeling of joy in me to have you sitting beside me on the journey to Inchbrook that day. How, with things going so well that day, I began to hope, began to plot, began to scheme to show you that I was not the perfect swine I'd up to then been with you.'

'Had—had you—er—planned to marry me then?' asked Keely, her heart going like a trip hammer.

'I was more determined than planning on that particular issue,' said Tarrant, to her great joy. 'To discover the very next morning that we'd started a child together was a very big plus as far as I was concerned. No need then, as I saw it, to have to carefully woo you, to get you to see me in a better light. To my way of thinking we could be married straight away, and from there on I would show you that I wasn't always the disbelieving swine you'd seen. Only,' his look was rueful, 'I'd accused you of too many outrageous things for you to marry me just like that, hadn't I?'

'I couldn't marry you,' she said quietly, 'when I was sure it was just from a point of honour that you were willing to give up your freedom.'

'I'll willingly give up what freedom I have, sweet Keely,' said Tarrant, his eyes tender on her, 'if only you'll say the word.' Confessing then, 'I hung around in the hall that morning waiting to hear you come from your room, intending then to tell you that whether there was a baby on the way or whether there wasn't, it made no difference.'

'But you—didn't!'

'The moment I saw you with your case in your hand, every thought went out of my head save that it didn't look as if it was going to be as simple as I'd hoped. I knew then that you were intent on leaving, that as far

as you were concerned, that was the last time I was
going to see you. I couldn't have that.'

'So you chose to drive me back to my flat,' Keely
took up. But as she remembered what had happened,
her eyes widened again as, still feeling the horror of that
occasion, she exclaimed, 'I thought you were going to
kill me that Sunday!'

'If it's any small consolation, I was afterwards
equally terrified,' he admitted, letting her know that he
had not missed seeing her terror. 'It frightened the life
out of me that, loving you with every breath, jealousy
should send me into such an intensity of rage to hear
you dare to state that you might marry someone else,
that I should want to harm you. That's why I couldn't
return that Sunday as I wanted. It scared the daylights
out of me that, loving you as I do, I might again be
visited by that same fury and might end up harming
you.'

Remembering that he had been on the phone first
thing the next morning when, having cooled down, he
must have felt more in control, Keely was amazed at his
depth of feeling for her. Yet she was still to question:

'You—love me?'

'That is precisely what I've been trying to tell you, my
sweet darling,' Tarrant said gently.

Joy took off in her to rocket skywards. Understanding
in her of how because of the depression that had been
in her, but was there no longer, Tarrant had taken his
time to gently get her to see how it was with him. But
with her eyes giving away that there was no need any
longer for him to go carefully, the shine in her eyes not
from sad thoughts, to her delight, he went on to tell her
just how much she meant to him.

'I can't live without you, my Keely,' he said, 'and
that's a plain fact. Without you my life is without
living. Work means nothing without you in my life.
High days, holidays, are without meaning,' he told her.
And there was no doubting that he meant every word

as he went on, 'You consume me so that you're my
world. I know you can't love me yet—God knows I've
done nothing to earn myself anything but your hate—
my last accusation topping the lot, but the fact that we
once started a new life between us must mean
something, don't you think?'

She nodded, and, her heart full, she just could not
hold back from telling him, 'But—I do already love
you, Tarrant.' And with emotion choking him as a dull
colour came up under his skin, she took her fingers
from his clasp and raised her hand until it rested on his
shoulder. 'I thought you knew that,' she whispered
softly.

For long moments Tarrant looked incredulously into
her eyes. But her eyes were hiding nothing. There for
him to see was the way she felt about him. And oh, how
good it was when, with a murmured exclamation, she
felt him gather her to him.

Oh, how good to feel his mouth over hers, saluting
her with tiny kisses. To be held away, then to find as he
gathered her to him again, that away was not where
Tarrant wanted her, but that he had just had to check
to see that that love look was still there in her eyes.

His kiss deepened. And one kiss never enough for
either of them, soon they were lying side by side,
wrapped in each other's arms, Keely's blood temperature soaring as Tarrant's longing for her made itself
known in those lengthening kisses.

'How long have you known?' he asked, his hands
caressing her as if he needed to touch her to assure
himself that to have her in his arms was not just some
wild, wonderful dream.

Keely didn't hold back. 'Since the first time you came
to my flat,' she told him.

'Since then!' His amazement was there for her to see
as, his voice thick, he asked, 'You knew when we made
love?'

'You didn't have to—er—force me, did you?' she

teased, glorying in the freedom that came with knowing that he loved her.

'Neither I did,' he smiled, and kissed her again with a passion that left her with very little clear thinking—though with just enough to have her putting a restraining hand on his chest.

When she went to sit up, though it was touch and go that she would not have lain down again had he asked her, she was to find that Tarrant was sitting too, an anxious note in his voice as he asked:

'Darling, what's wr . . .' He broke off, and she knew again that his brain had gone to question that which he did not know. For his voice was infinitely gentle, even if he had come up with the wrong answer, when his arms came to hold her tenderly as he said, 'Give me the right to keep you in my arms, sweet Keely. Even if things aren't well with you yet, marry me soon. I'll wait as long as I have to to touch you again, but I must have the right to hold you sleeping in my arms through the night.'

'It's—not that,' she answered shyly, marvelling at the depth of tenderness in him.

'Then what, sweetheart?' he asked gently. 'Is there something I should have explained and haven't?'

Hoping he would remain understanding, that he would stay gentle, that he would keep his patience with her, Keely sought for words.

'It's——' she began. 'Well——' she faltered. And taking a deep breath, she told him, 'Before—before when I wouldn't agree to marry you—it was because my getting myself pregnant was exactly what you'd forecast I was out to do—my way of trapping you into marriage. But I'm not pregnant now, nor do I want to be until—I'm married.'

'Until *we're* married,' he corrected, murmuring as his arms tightened about her, 'My God, I hurt you badly didn't I, my darling?'

'That's all over,' she said quickly, and for her it was; her forgiveness was complete.

'But what your saying now is—hands off until you have my ring on your finger?'

'Don't accuse me of blackmail,' Keely begged, her eyes damp and shining as she looked at him. 'It's just that it—scares me that I can conceive so easily. I'd somehow got the idea that—couples had to try for ages.'

'Oh, my beloved girl,' said Tarrant, his love laid bare for her to see. 'Stop being afraid. If there's been any use of blackmail, it's been I who have used it. I was prepared to use any means, even that beginning we started, if it meant I could get you to be my wife.'

'I'm sorry,' she said huskily.

'It's I who am sorry,' he told her tenderly. 'Never will I ever accuse you of anything again. I love you, my sweet Keely,' he said. 'I need you. I just can't take any more of this emptiness in me without you. Marry me, and let me prove to you that the beast I once was with you has ceased to exist?'

'Oh, Tarrant,' Keely smiled, 'I love you so, and you know that I'll marry you whenever you say.'

'Thank God for that,' he said on a heartfelt prayer.

But when, never happier, Keely just could do no other than reveal that happiness in her smiling eyes, her upward curving mouth, Tarrant could not deny his need to kiss her again.

And as before, she soon found that she was again being pressed to the mattress, Tarrant kissing her so thoroughly that, her response being all he could wish for, passion was again stirring. A passion which this time she found she had no defence against, nor did she have any protest to make when his caresses had her mindless with wanting.

When abruptly he left off caressing her, and at the same time took his mouth away from hers, then got up from the bed pulling her with him, the only protest Keely wanted to make was that they should return to the way they had been.

Her face flushed from his lovemaking, what she was feeling there in her eyes, she heard Tarrant's voice, gruff and strained when, looking down at her, he said:

'We'd better go and tell the parents.'

'Do we—have to—*now*?' she asked huskily.

Her answer was to have him pulling her with him to the door. 'My God, do you do something to a man's self-control,' she heard him mutter. 'Yes, Keely Macfarlane, we do,' he said, firmly pushing her out in front of him through the door. 'But just you wait until you're Mrs Tarrant Varley,' he threatened.

Keely giggled, and once they were safely the other side of her bedroom door, Tarrant could not resist a kiss to the tip of her dainty nose.

'It won't be long now,' she said, giving him a loving look.

'I'll make damn sure of that,' he growled, the burning look in his grey eyes revealing the truth of that.

By the time they had reached the bottom of the stairs, they were both grinning idiotically, arms around each other, so that when Catherine and Lucas, as if they had been waiting to hear them, came to stand watching them, Lucas after just one look at them turned to beam at his wife.

'By the look on my son's face, my dear,' he said, 'I think you'd better shake the dust off your best hat.'

And as Catherine too beamed, and looked from Lucas back to where Tarrant still had tight hold of Keely, 'From the look on my daughter's face,' she replied, as together they went to embrace them, 'I think maybe I better had.'

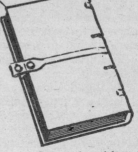

Take these
best-selling
4 novels
FREE

Yes! Four sophisticated, contemporary love stories by four world-famous authors of romance FREE, as your introduction to the Harlequin Presents subscription plan. Thrill to **Anne Mather**'s passionate story BORN OUT OF LOVE, set in the Caribbean.... Travel to darkest Africa in **Violet Winspear**'s TIME OF THE TEMPTRESS....Let **Charlotte Lamb** take you to the fascinating world of London's Fleet Street in MAN'S WORLD ....Discover beautiful Greece in **Sally Wentworth**'s moving romance SAY HELLO TO YESTERDAY.

The very finest in romance fiction

Join the millions of avid Harlequin readers all over the world who delight in the magic of a really exciting novel. EIGHT great NEW titles published EACH MONTH! Each month you will get to know exciting, interesting, true-to-life people .... You'll be swept to distant lands you've dreamed of visiting .... Intrigue, adventure, romance, and the destiny of many lives will thrill you through each Harlequin Presents novel.

Get all the latest books before they're sold out!
As a Harlequin subscriber you actually receive your personal copies of the latest Presents novels immediately after they come off the press, so you're sure of getting all 8 each month.

Cancel your subscription whenever you wish!
You don't have to buy any minimum number of books. Whenever you decide to stop your subscription just let us know and we'll cancel all further shipments.

Your **FREE** gift includes

Anne Mather—Born out of Love
Violet Winspear—Time of the Temptress
Charlotte Lamb—Man's World
Sally Wentworth—Say Hello to Yesterday